QUICK ON THE DRAW

Detained for a crime he had not committed, Glenister McCreedie is released on parole from prison. However, later that night, Glenister finds himself with a dead prison guard on his hands, and he flees to the railway construction town of Keedie. There his past catches up with him and he's forced to break his parole as he confronts brutal mule skinners and fights cattle thieves and train robbers.

ALAN HOLMES

QUICK ON THE DRAW

Complete and Unabridged

LINFORD
Leicester

First published in Great Britain in 1953

First Linford Edition
published 2010

British Library CIP Data

Holmes, Alan.
    Quick on the draw. - -
    (Linford western library)
    1. Western stories.
    2. Large type books.
    I. Title II. Series
    823.9′14–dc22

    ISBN 978–1–44480–089–0

Published by
F. A. Thorpe (Publishing)
Anstey, Leicestershire

Set by Words & Graphics Ltd.
Anstey, Leicestershire
Printed and bound in Great Britain by
T. J. International Ltd., Padstow, Cornwall

This book is printed on acid-free paper

1

The shrewd, friendly, brown eyes of the Warden of Rocky Point Penitentiary looked from the papers on his desk into the steely blue eyes of the prisoner standing before him. The man was powerfully built and the grotesque, badly fitting convict garb of yellow and black could not conceal his fine physique.

Glenister McCreedie at the age of twenty-five was in the prime of life. Weighing a hundred and ninety pounds and standing six foot one, he was a model of magnificent healthy manhood. In that fine body a force of pent-up emotion strained against the fetters that restrained it — emotion that had been growing over a period of three years. Three years spent behind stone walls and iron bars — the wildest tiger in a steel cage. Here was restrained energy, waiting and watching, with a ferocity that knew no bounds, for the moment when those fetters would be snapped.

The Warden was a good judge of his fellow humans — he had to be in his job. He knew of the hidden fires of hate that smouldered in this man's soul. Hate against the law and hate against the society that had created the law. Of all the prisoners who had passed through his hands, he felt McCreedie was the most dangerous. Yet never once throughout the three years of his sentence had he committed the slightest breach of the strict rules which were enforced in the toughest penitentiary in the West. His fellow prisoners — hardened criminals, killers serving life sentences — all respected and feared this soft-spoken youngster.

For a moment their eyes held, then the Warden's dropped to the papers in front of him.

'I have some good news for you, McCreedie. Your courage and leadership on the occasion of the fire in Block

Two a couple of months ago did not go unnoticed by me. Acting on my report the Governor has been pleased to grant you parole as a reward for your loyalty.'

For a second a flicker of pleasure showed in McCreedie's eyes, but not a muscle of his face moved. The Warden continued:

'You will realize the great generosity with which the Governor has acted. There are few instances where a prisoner has been granted parole after serving only three years of a ten years' sentence. I have here the details of your trial and I notice that you persisted in your statement that you were not present at the time of the Bank hold-up. Nevertheless the jury of twelve men found you guilty and the judge sentenced you accordingly. It is not for me to make any comment.'

McCreedie spoke for the first time. 'What I said at the trial was true. I weren't within twenty miles of Ogden the day of the hold-up.'

'The jury appeared to think differently.'

'I tell you, Warden, the same as I told them — I was framed.'

'Knowing you as I do, I believe you and that brings me to my next point, which I cannot emphasize too strongly. One of the conditions of your parole is that you do not carry a gun in the State of Utah.' McCreedie jumped — the Warden held up his hand. 'Let me finish. If you carry a gun your parole will be revoked and you will find yourself back behind these walls. Now, McCreedie, I do not want that to happen. Brought up with firearms from childhood, like all Westerners and moving among men who wear a gun as naturally as they wear a hat, I appreciate how you must feel about this condition. But it is a condition of your parole and one that must be fulfilled.'

'I reckon whoever had that there condition put in knew what he had in mind. But for a fella like me it's a one-way ticket to Boothill. Every tinhorn gambler and imitation badman looking for fame will be out gunning for Glenister McCreedie. What chance am I goin' to have?'

'That's fool talk, McCreedie, and you know it. The West's a big place and it's developing every day. There are thousands of places where the name of McCreedie's never been heard. With your knowledge of horses and stock you can earn a living anywhere and once you're out of the state the condition does not apply.'

A bitter twist came to McCreedie's lips. 'Yer know, Warden, fer a fella I've gotten a great respect fer, you ain't very conversant with the way the badge toters uphold this 'ere law yer talking about once yer get out to the ranges and foothills. When I leave here I figger the sheriff back home will be told I've been released?'

'Certainly. And many others. That, too, is a condition of your parole.'

'Shore I knowed it. The sheriff back

home never did cotton to us McCreedies, so he tells his cronies and afore yer
know where yer are the whole blamed
country knows I ain't supposed to pack
a gun and down will come the wolves
howling fer ma blood. Inside a month it
will be common talk in every saloon
from here to Nevada — and you say
'move out'. I figger I'll have to be on
the move all the time savin' ma neck or
I'll be planted in Boothill. Any old how
I figger it ain't any o' your doin' and
I'm mighty grateful fer what yer dun fer
me.'

He stuck out his hand and the
Warden shook it warmly.

'You'll make out, fella.'

'When do I leave?'

'Tomorrow, come sun-up.'

'Thanks fer all yer dun, Warden. So
long.'

The midday break was in progress
when McCreedie got back to the
exercise yard. Selecting a sunny spot by
the wall he squatted, cowboy fashion,
on his heels. The Warden's news had

come as a great surprise to him and he wanted time to think it over. As a privileged prisoner he was allowed to smoke and he automatically fished out the makings and rolled himself a cigarette. Freedom! The very word made him want to pinch himself to be sure that he had not dreamed it. But to be denied a gun! To be free and walk about without the weight of a gun on his thigh was like asking him to walk about naked. His thoughts were roaming on the sage-covered uplands of the high mesa country when 'Luny', the feeble-minded lifer, shuffled up.

'Hi there, Glen. Gotta smoke fer a guy?'

McCreedie tossed him the sack of Durhams.

'What the ol' man want yer for?'

'Who told yer the Warden wanted me?'

The old man shrugged his shoulders. 'I heard Big Shot Finney a-talking.'

Glenister's face darkened.

'Now don't get sore with me. Yer

7

knows there ain't much that goes on in this place that there guy don't know about.'

'I ain't sore with you, Luny, but I don't cotton kindly to other folks poking into my business.'

'I figger he's headin' this way right now.'

A short ferret-like man of about forty had detached himself from a crowd at the other end of the yard and was making in their direction. He scowled at Luny.

'Scram, you bum. I want to talk to McCreedie.'

The feeble-minded lifer glared at him venomously but made no reply and shuffled off.

'Never can understand how a guy like you can put up with that stool pigeon hanging around.'

Glenister smiled wryly. 'He's harmless enough. What's eating yer, Finney? Knowing yer as I do, I don't reckon yer'd honour me with yer company just to talk about old Luny.'

'I'll come down to cases right away — so yer on yer way out, are yer? I reckon a good guy like you deserves it.'

'There ain't much around that yer don't know, is there, Finney?'

'I reckon not. A guy in my position's gotta. Mebbe you and me ain't seen things the same way in the past, but I figger I owes yer a lot for saving my life in that there fire a piece back. When Larry Finney owes a debt he pays it and I aim to do that right now. Yer got no dough and a guy outside without dough's got no chance. My friends can use a guy with your reputation as a gun-slinger. Yer mabbe don't know it, but I'm labour recruiting boss in these parts for the railroad and that organization can use a guy like you in the construction camps. These greenhorn Irishmen are tough babies when they're in likker and it needs a tough guy to handle 'em. Yer the man for the job. The pay's good — all yer gotta do is take a note I'll give yer to Val Mooney's saloon here in town. He'll give yer an

9

advance against yer first month's pay and a chit to the boss. Then yer can climb aboard a construction train right away. How d'yer feel about it?'

Glenister studied this boss gambler with the political pulls. Even here, behind bars, his influence was amazing. Guards were bribed and anyone who got in his way or disagreed with him was conveniently removed and the process of removal did not stop at murder.

'What's the strings attached to this generosity o' yourn?'

'Doggorn it, McCreedie, can't a guy help a guy that saved his neck? There ain't no strings and possibly when I get out o' here — and that won't be long — I can put more in yer way.'

'Mebbe I've figgered yer wrong, Finney. I ain't ever met a fella like yer afore. But get this straight — I was framed into here and when I get out I aim to go straight. That is if those law buzzards'll let me. If they don't it'll be too bad.'

Finney laughed scornfully, 'Pull yer neck in, fella. Don't yer realize that once yer've been in the pen there's allus some buzzard ready to squeal on yer? They'll never give yer a chance and the first chance they get some blamed badge toter will frame a charge on yer and yer'll be hauled back to finish yer sentence. There's only one way and that's to work with the high-ups that make the laws. It's all graft and they're the biggest grafters of all. They pay good dough for the work they want dun and they'll protect yer into the bargain. Just the same as they'll have yer rubbed out if yer get in their way.'

'I reckon this 'ere protection misfired in your case, else yer wouldn't be here.'

'That was an accident that couldn't be covered up. But don't you worry — the high-ups are already working for my release. Anyhow, d'yer accept my offer or don't yer? I tells yer there's no strings.'

'A fella that's as broke as I am can't pick and choose. Write yer note and I'll see this Mooney fella gets it.'

'Yer a good guy, Glen. Stick with us and yer'll be in the real dough in no time. I'll tell Mooney to give yer the coin. So long, fella, I guess it won't be long before we meet outside.'

Glenister watched him walk across the yard and rejoin the crap game. Range raised as he was these slick city grafters had him buffaloed. Anyway, what had he to lose? Even the warden had yapped glibly about going further West — perhaps working for this railroad outfit might be the solution. Shucks, he must be loco! He was a range rider, a bronc peeler, a cowhand, anything but one of these spike bashers or muck slingers. He laughed quietly and cynically. A cowhand without a bronc or a gun and, as far as he could remember, about fifteen bucks to his name. Beggars couldn't be choosers — he'd see what this Finney proposition was like. One thing — it would get him out of town and miles from the pen, and the further he got from that the better he'd like it.

Somewhere in his mind a third sense warned him to beware of Finney and from past experience this third sense of his had seldom been wrong.

The bell was ringing for the resumption of work. He got slowly to his feet. To think that this time tomorrow he would be free! He made his way back into the workshop. From his locker he drew out a horsehair bridle — it was a beautiful job and had taken him months of patient work. He took out a hand-tooled holster and a gunbelt — these too, he had made himself. What was the use of them? A bridle when you hadn't got a horse and a holster when you hadn't got a gun! He bundled them up in a piece of sacking — they couldn't stop him taking them out, anyway.

He started to finish the job he'd been doing when he'd been called to the Warden's office. Preoccupied by his thoughts and work he did not see Gorman, one of the guards, until he stood over him. Glenister did not like this smug bully.

'So they're lettin' yer go?' was his opening remark.

'Yeah. Ain't it too bad fer yer? Or mebbe yer pleased? Without me around yer'll be able to bully and bash the life out o' my pard Luny. Yer know, Gorman, if there's one thing I hates back home it's a rattler. And wors'n a rattler — two rattlers. I figger yer lower than a rattler.'

The guard's face became a mask of hate.

'Go on — use the blackjack yer carrying. Yer darn't 'cos yer knows that after tomorrow I'd be waiting fer yer when yer come out. And I'd give yer what yer've given these poor devils fer years. One of these days we might meet up outside and then, by crikey, I'll settle a few scores.'

'What yer got in that bundle?'

'That's my business. Are yer aiming on taking a look?'

Their eyes met and held for a second

or two. Then the guard quit and turned away.

'Yaller, as I always thought,' muttered Glen to himself.

As they lined up for chuck one of Finney's stooges slipped a note into his hand. The cage door clanged and the key turned on him for the last time. Come what may in the future, he thought, never should they put him behind bars again.

His cell mate was old Luny. The other prisoners had marvelled at his accepting the half-wit to share his cage and it had not escaped the notice of the Warden and the chief guard — nor, for that matter, of Gorman, who had previously found the old man an easy prey for his brutalities.

It was after one such brutal beating that Glen had made up his mind to protect him. In Luny he saw twenty-five years of captivity behind bars. Maybe it was true that in a brainstorm he had murdered his nagging wife, but surely after all these years he had paid for his crime. Luny had been an engineer and Glenister had grown used to his ramblings about the great turbine he was going to build and encouraged him to talk.

Tonight the old fellow ate his chuck in silence — something was on his mind.

Glenister took the note from his pocket and in cupped hands, read its contents:

VAL.

THIS IS GLENISTER MCCREEDIE. I RECKON HIS GUNS MIGHT COME IN USEFUL TO O'LEARY. GIVE HIM A COUPLA HUNDRED BUCKS AND ARRANGE FOR HIM TO GET ABOARD A CONSTRUCTION FREIGHT CAR TO KEEDIE.

FINNEY.

There was nothing much wrong with that except that the great Finney was apparently not aware of the parole condition about carrying a gun. Two hundred bucks — not enough to buy a horse, but better than nothing.

Luny had finished eating and was staring with downcast eyes at the bundle containing the bridle and holster. Suddenly, without a word, he got up and went over to his bunk.

For some time he stood picking at the stitching on one corner of the mattress until he had made a hole large enough to get his hand inside. He pulled out a bundle of bills. It was not a large roll.

Hesitantly he proffered it to Glen. 'I reckon you'll need this now yer goin' out. I saved it for the day when I was released, but I reckon they means to keep me here till the undertaker comes fer me. Take it, son. Better yer should have it than that buzzard Gorman. He's shore to take it off me when yer gone.'

A lump came into Glen's throat. For a few moments he could only sit and stare at the roll of bills. The edges were singed and charred. For the life of him he could not find words. The old man's generosity dumbfounded him.

'How come they been burnt, Luny?'

'It were this roll I were after when I went back into the cage — you remember when we had the fire and you bawled me out.'

'Doggorn it. So that's what yer were after. And yer told me it were them plans fer yer turbine! Put 'em back, Luny, where yer got 'em from. I'm mighty grateful fer the offer, but yer'll need that coin mor'n me when yer get out.'

'No, Glen. I'll never get out o' here alive. I can feel it in these old bones o' mine and I'd be mighty proud fer yer to take the coin.'

'Now, Luny, do as I say. Put those bills back in that there hide-out and stop all this blather about not gettin' out o' here alive. Look at me — last night I was here for another seven years and now I'm out come sun-up. That's what's goin' to happen to yer one of these days, and then I'll come and fetch yer and show yer them mountains I dun told yer about, with rushing rivers and great waterfalls, where yer can build that there turbine yer always talking about and the water can drive it.'

A new light came into the old man's eyes — he was once more the engineer.

'Tell me again about the mountains, Glen.'

'Put that coin away and then I will.'

Gently and patiently Glen repeated the oft-told tale of the great mountains and the rivers. It was little enough to do for this unfortunate, condemned to spend the rest of his few remaining years behind bars.

2

The bright sun had barely had time to warm the sidewalks of the city when the great gates opened and clanged behind Glenister McCreedie. He was free. Free to go and come as he pleased. To meet people — see things — to feel the biting wind of a north-easter on his face or the hot summer sun. To roll himself in his blankets and gaze at the stars or listen to the mournful cry of the coyotes. Never again should they fence him in — never.

What a difference it made to one's feelings to be wearing one's own clothes — the confidence it gave. You were no longer a number wearing yellow and black sacking — ordered here and there — herded together like a lot of cattle.

The sedate and demure Mormon housewives out on their early morning shopping expeditions, stared with curious and admiring eyes from beneath their prim bonnets, at this finely developed range rider as he strode along the sidewalk. He wore the clothes he had been wearing at the time of his arrest — a faded blue shirt, blue jeans tucked into hand-tooled high-heeled riding boots, large rowelled Mexican spurs that tinkled as he trailed them in the dust. Over his shirt a black calfskin vest and around his neck a yellow bandanna. A huge, almost white, sombrero was cocked jauntily to one side of his head.

He was a typical range rider, but an acute observer would have noticed the absence of a gun and the pallor of his skin in striking contrast to the weather-beaten tan of the normal cowboy. His gait, too, was a little clumsy — he was finding his high-heeled boots both tight and difficult to walk in after the heavy flat-heeled prison issue.

There was only one thing in his mind as he ambled down the street, and that was a real good meal. He had been handed seventeen dollars on his release — all the money which he had on him when he was taken to jail — and it was burning a hole in his pocket. He wanted a steak covered with onions and a couple of eggs on it and lashings of coffee.

He spotted an eating-house which described itself as 'Daisy's Kitchen' and in no time he had dodged the rigs and freight wagons which were already ploughing their way through the ankle-deep dust.

A non-too-clean frousty blonde took his order and despite the dinginess of the place he did full justice to the cooking.

The frousty blonde watched him in amazement. Never before had she seen a customer put away so much food in so short a time. As for coffee, it was not until he'd finished his sixth cup that he decided to give his digestive organs a little time to get accustomed to normal food.

Calling for his check, he strolled out and stood contentedly leaning against the hitching-rail watching the traffic pass and re-pass.

Folks hadn't changed much, though there were more of them — a heap more. The men were the same predominating sober-faced Mormons in their black and dark grey store suits. These 'Latter Day Saints' were grim and hardy, little given to any form of gaiety or laughter — scorning the frivolities of life.

But the coming of the railroad had also brought the flotsam and jetsam of the world to this once exclusively Mormon settlement. Up and down its crowded sidewalks went miners, cowhands, fancy-waistcoated gamblers, wide-eyed carpet baggers. Men from the mountains and the ranges.

In the streets, cursing and sweating mule skinners and bull whackers yelled at their teams as they hauled their huge wagons filled with stores through the deep ruts. Women were there too. The bonneted Mormon housewife rubbed shoulders with painted dance-hall girls wearing their exaggerated bustles which bobbed and wobbled with every step they took — their parasols nearly poked out a fella's eyes as they passed.

Horses were everywhere and of every type — from the fancy-saddled ponies of the cowboys to the expensive high-stepping thoroughbreds in rigs and buggies. The everyday hard-worked bronc and the heavier work horses in buck-boards and wagons passed in endless procession before his eyes.

There were more buildings — bigger and better buildings, some of them of stone. Some of the stores had extra large windows the better to display their wares — good targets for the likkered-up cowhand to shoot out when he was on a drunk.

One of these new windows caught Glenister's eye. It was that of the saddler and harness maker. In its centre was a beautiful saddle — one that would enrapture any range rider. Hand made of the best hogskin, it had gleaming conches of ivory and a reinforced horn for roping. He looked at the price ticket — a hundred and eighty bucks. Not much if you said it quick, but a fortune to him with less than sixteen dollars in his jeans. He sighed and examined a couple of halters hanging on a peg by the door, then he walked on.

He came to the gunsmith's. Here were the old-time frontier 44's, a Remington repeater rifle and a pair of English shotguns in a case; he had never seen their like before. Longingly he examined every detail, even to the everyday pull-through.

He stood looking for so long that the owner of the shop came out and asked him what he would like to see.

Glenister thanked him, mumbled something about returning later and walked on.

He remembered Finney's note and enquiring from a passerby where he could find Mooney's Saloon, was directed to go two blocks further on.

He found himself getting into the down-town part of the city. The stone buildings gave way to wooden framework shacks. Even at this comparatively early hour honky-tonk music reached his ear. This was the district of saloons and dance halls.

No one could have missed the huge garish sign that adorned the whole length of a building informing the world that it was 'MOONEY'S — THE HOME OF THE IRISH'.

Glenister pushed open the swing door and let his eyes roam around the large room. There appeared to be no shortage of customers. A number of men stood at the bar and gambling was in progress at several tables. A group in one corner were playing crap. Most of the company were of the carpet-bagger type — emigrants newly arrived from Europe.

He walked over to the bar and called for a bourbon. The bartender eyed him up and down without speaking and then slid a bottle and glass across the polished counter.

Glen helped himself and put down a silver dollar. 'Where'd I find the boss?' he asked.

'Who wants to know?' came the surly reply.

'I've gotta note for him from a friend.'

The bartender called over to a broken-nosed individual — obviously a bouncer. 'Pitcher, there's a guy here says he's a note for the boss.'

Pitcher leered at him. 'It's early for the boss to see anyone. Who's the note from?'

'Finney,' drawled Glen. The name acted like magic.

'Why'd yer not say so at first? Follow me.' He pushed open a door alongside the bar.

Glenister followed him closely and found himself face to face with a big raw-boned man in the forties, seated with his feet up on a desk, reading a paper. He glared at Pitcher and cursed.

'How many more times am I to tell yer I ain't to be disturbed when I'm readin' the paper?'

'This guy says he gotta note fer yer from Finney.'

The man jumped at the mention of the name. 'Finney, did yer say? Now yer wouldn't be kiddin' a fella, would yer, mister? When would yer be seein' Finney?'

'Yesterday afternoon.'

'Where?'

'In the pen.'

'Get out, Pitcher, and stay out till I calls fer yer.' He hitched over a chair with the toe of his boot. 'Sit down, stranger. Lets be seein' the note.'

Glen took the note from his shirt pocket and tossed it on to the table. There was something about this hombre he didn't like.

Mooney unfolded it — read it and stuck out a podgy white hand. On one finger was a diamond the size of a dime. 'Glad to know yer, McCreedie. I'm figgerin' yer just got out.'

Glenister took the hand and out of sheer spite squeezed it in his mighty grip — Mooney winced.

'Yer figger right.'

'Shore, shore,' he shook his fingers. 'I guess yer ain't lost none o' that strength o' yourn up there. Big Shot tells me to give yer a couple o' hundred bucks and arrange fer yer to get aboard the construction train tonight.'

'I read the note.'

Mooney pulled out a huge roll from his pocket and peeled off two one-hundred-dollar bills.

Glenister picked them up. 'Got any small for one of these?'

'Shore, anything to oblige, McCreedie. How d'yer like it — in tens or twenties?'

'Tens'll do.'

Mooney opened a desk drawer and from another large roll gave him the change.

'Much obliged.'

'It's a pleasure. Yer goin' to like O'Leary — a good guy is Paddy and as Big Shot says, I reckon he'll be able to use yer guns to help him keep order.'

'Is there much trouble up at Keedie? I've never been in that neck o' the woods.'

'No more than yer'd find in any other railroad camp. O'Leary's a hellion with his fists but nary a bit o' good with a gun. That's where Big Shot's figgerin' on you comin' in, I guess. But let's have a drink. I'll show yer over the place and yer can make yerself welcome till the train pulls out. I figger we got quite a few already that'll be aboard her, but I'll introduce yer to the train boss later.'

They left the office and went over to the bar.

'Give me my special bottle, Tim.' Mooney poured out two generous measures and handed one to Glen. 'Here's to the railroad — yes, the railroad. This country owes a lot to the railroad and them that builds it.'

Mooney's manner had entirely changed and for a moment Glenister could not think what had come over him — and then he realized that the man was talking for the benefit of other customers in the bar.

He must have shown his bewilderment for a second, for Mooney half closed one eye at him and then went on with his loud talk.

'I arrived in this 'ere new country nigh on thirty years ago with my folks from Cork. My ole man hadn't mor'n a few shillings in his pocket and look at him today with his own ranch and me with this 'ere saloon — and we both got 'em by working on the railroad. There's big dough waiting fer any guy who's willin' to work with the railroads.'

'How could yer get on if yer knew nothing about railroads?' asked a carpet bagger standing near by.

Mooney laughed. 'Anyone can work fer that outfit — it's brawn yer want, not brains. Guys that can swing a sledge and use a pick and shovel — them's the ones that makes the coin.'

'How's a chap get on with wife and kids?' asked another.

'Take 'em with yer. There's room fer all out there — ain't there, Glen?' He turned towards his questioners: 'This fella's from the ranges — he knows.'

'I figger ther's plenty o' room if nort else.'

'How d'yer get there?' asked the man who'd first spoken.

'Get a ticket from the company's agent. He'll be here tonight. The train leaves the depot at midnight. All yer gotta do is climb aboard and it'll take yer right to the job. Come on, fellas, belly up. The house is buyin' and we'll drink to the railroad in a drop o' real Irish whiskey I've shipped from the ould country. Tell me if yer can't taste the smokey tang o' the peat.'

The men crowded forward and Glen took the opportunity to wander away.

Mooney continued his blarney about the golden opportunities offered by work with the railroad and Glenister began to realize what Finney had meant when he said there was big dough to be had by working for the high-ups.

Mooney's racket was plain — plenty of cheap liquor and a good tale and the emigrant woke up to find himself in a construction gang miles away in the wilds. With no money and no transport he'd have to stay on the job whether he liked it or not.

Mooney and his gang, he suspected, got paid for every recruit they sent along. Shanghai-ing was the proper name for it.

For a time he watched the poker and monte players, then he drifted over to the crap game. It was obvious that the tinhorn running the game was milking the greenhorns who'd probably never before seen a dice in their lives.

He stood quietly watching the game — the bills were burning a hole in his pocket and his fingers fairly itched to join in the game. He had played crap since he'd been knee high and the barefaced robbery that was going on made his blood boil. He moved closer to the table.

The gambler noticed his interest.

'Fancy a roll, cowboy?'

'Shore do,' Glen drawled, 'if we can play with the house bones.'

The gambler scowled. 'What d'yer mean by that, fella?'

'Nothin'. Just fancy the house dice.'

The other players were curious — the gambler was cornered and he knew it. He had either to agree or back down — the latter was impossible. 'Bring us the house dice, Pitcher,' he yelled.

The bouncer brought over the dice and mumbled something into the tinhorn's ear. From the looks the latter cast at McCreedie it was clear that Pitcher had been informing him of his identity.

He picked up the dice and holding them close to his ear in his closed fists shook and rattled them.

'What d'yer call, cowboy? Yer kin start.'

'I'll go fer ten,' said Glen, laying down one of his ten-dollar bills.

The gambler threw down the dice and Glenister picked them up. At his first throw he threw a natural — he threw again — a two and a five. He had made it.

'I reckon yer luck's in, fella. Lettin' it ride fer twenty?'

'Shore.'

For the next five throws he won again and there was now six hundred and thirty dollars on the table. All play at the other tables had stopped and players and spectators, including Mooney, crowded around.

The gambler had lost his calm — he was a ruffled man. This cowhand sure had him buffaloed — ' poker-face' was not in it — those steel grey eyes never batted a lid. 'Yer goin' again, fella?' he asked huskily, glancing anxiously at the saloon keeper who made no sign.

'Why not? I allus believe in a fella following his luck when it's in.'

It was the gambler's turn to roll 'em and Glen's eyes never left the man's hands — he was out of luck and finished with a nine.

Though Glen picked up the ivories

35

calmly enough, he was inwardly on fire. If he won this time it would mean twelve hundred and sixty dollars — sufficient for a stake to start him on a new life. A quick flip and the small white cubes went skimming over the table — a six — the other wobbled undecidedly for a second and Glen's heart stood still — the dice flopped over — ONE! Again he'd made it.

With a curse the gambler called for more money. Mooney supplied it from a wad he pulled from his pocket — he threw it on the table.

Glen collected it slowly. 'Thanks, gents. I reckon I've had enough fer one day. I can't expect my luck to last fer ever.'

'Why, dang yer,' shouted the gambler. 'Yer mean ter say yer're quittin'? Like hell yer are.' His hand dived into his vest but before he could withdraw it Glen's fist cracked him on the jaw. His eyes glazed and he would have fallen, but Glen caught him by the lapels of his coat with his left hand. At the same time he slipped his right into the man's coat and brought out a small Derringer.

'A nasty toy,' he drawled, looking at the deadly weapon that lay in his hand. He let the body slump to the floor and threw the gun on the table.

'Give it to him when he wakes up. Sorry to have caused a fracas in yer house, Mooney. I'll see yer tonight as arranged.'

Their eyes met for a second. 'I guess he had it comin',' was Mooney's reply.

Without pausing Glen walked out of the saloon.

'An' he weren't packin' a gun,' murmured Mooney to Pitcher, the bouncer. 'I reckon Finney shore hired himself a cool 'un this time.'

It was a very different Glenister who now strode purposely up the main street. When he had sauntered down in search of Mooney's saloon, three hours ago, he had seen no prospect of getting the things which were essential for his future. Now they were well within his reach.

His first visit was to the saddler. He bought the saddle which he had so greatly admired earlier in the day, a heavy silver curb bit, a lariat, pigging string and the other usual accoutrements of a range rider.

With a bed-roll and gunny bag under one arm and the saddle under the other he made his way to the gunsmiths. He had not forgotten the condition of his parole, but while he was not allowed to tote a gun there was no mention forbidding him to possess one. Furthermore there had been no specification of the gun he was not allowed to carry and a fellow had a right to a rifle on the range to protect himself from rattlers or to hunt food in order to live. Into his gunny bag went a brace of 44's, a rifle, a bowie knife and a box of shells.

With the gunsmith's friendly permission he left gunny bag and saddle in the shop while he went on to the clothing store where he rigged himself out with a complete outfit including slicker and storm jacket. He had, at last, got an outfit together and sundown found him at the railroad depot with all his purchases. He checked them with the booking agent and sauntered back into the town in search of more chuck.

He found an eating-house and over his meal and numerous cups of Java he pondered things out.

His luck in the crap game had been wonderful. After getting together his outfit, he still had enough money to buy a good horse and get a new start in life.

He felt he really owed it all to Finney — had he not given him the note for Mooney he would never have gone near the place. Still he had a feeling that somewhere behind Finney's apparent good will there was an underlying motive. What he had already seen of Mooney and his associates had left a bad taste in his mouth. Could it be that they wanted a hired gun-hand to protect this O'Leary and from what had this so-called construction boss to be protected? Surely not from a bunch of greenhorn Irish emigrants. Think as he would, he was at a loss to fathom their intentions. There was only one thing to do — play the cards as they fell.

He strolled leisurely back to Mooney's. The place had taken on an entirely different appearance. Outside kerosene flares blazed, lighting up the sign MOONEY's — THE HOME FOR THE IRISH. Women and children sat on bundles on the open feed lot as they waited for their menfolk inside the saloon. It looked like mass emigration on a small scale.

From inside came the singing of half-drunken men. Why was it, Glenister wondered, that folk taking up new homes in a land they did not know, always sang? It had been the same with the Mormon wagon trains he had seen in the past. But their singing had been of doleful hymns in striking contrast to the lively Irish tunes now coming from this saloon.

He pushed open the door and found the place so crowded that he had difficulty in making his way to the bar.

Those bound for the railroad were in a bunch by themselves — most of them appeared to be drunk and were either singing or laughing or squabbling amongst themselves.

Glenister stood for a moment taking stock of the scene. Shysters and tinhorns were relieving the poor fools of what little coin they had left. Patent medicine men were selling potions guaranteed to cure every type of fever or pestilence and lucky charms which insured the discovery of gold. If this sort of thing was customary, no wonder Finney and his cronies were growing rich.

Suddenly his eyes lighted on Gorman, the prison guard. So he, too, was a frequenter of Mooney's — that explained a lot. No wonder Finney had always been so well informed and been granted all privileges; he'd bet a dime to a dollar Gorman was in the grafter's pay.

He was playing poker and Glenister moved over to watch the game. From his manner he was apparently losing heavily. Glen saw him lose several pots and was on the verge of going in search of Mooney, when Gorman dived his hand into his pocket and brought out a bundle of bills.

Glen stiffened — he had seen that bundle before — the edges were scorched. It was the bundle Luny had produced from his mattress the night before. So he had robbed the old man.

He had always hated this bully and now he saw red. Here was the opportunity for which he had been waiting. He pushed past a couple of other men who had been watching the game and stood behind Gorman.

A nearer view of the bundle of bills confirmed him in the opinion that it was Luny's. Bending over Gorman's shoulder he whispered, 'I got something mighty particular I want ter talk ter yer about.'

Gorman started at the sound of his voice. He appeared to be taken a-back.

'What yer want?' he snarled. 'Can't yer see I'm busy?'

'Shore. But I'm pullin' out tonight and what I gotta say won't keep.'

Gorman got up from his chair, 'I'll be back,' he said to the players and followed Glen outside. As they reached a spot out of the lamplight Glenister spun round and grabbed the surprised Gorman.

'Where'd yer get that dough yer were playing in there with, fella? Talk and talk fast if yer don't want to get the biggest beating of yer life.'

'Why, you bastard,' gasped Gorman as he struggled to get free. 'So you aim to rob me, do yer?'

He got no further — Glen's fist crashed into his mouth. 'Talk, fella, if yer know what's good fer yer.'

'I'll see yer in hell first,' came through Gorman's clenched teeth and bleeding mouth.

Another blow and another. 'I aim ter make yer,' panted Glen, beside himself with rage at the theft of the old man's money.

Gorman's head was reeling and he

went down under an avalanche of blows. Glen hauled him to his feet, stuck him up against the wall and swung him round at the same time — there was the sharp crack of a gun. Glen felt a bullet skim his ear and heard Gorman grunt as it hit him. There was the sound of running steps and then only the distant noise from the saloon. Gorman was falling.

For a second Glen did not realize what had happened and then it swept over him in a whirl — Gorman was dead. But had the bullet been intended for him himself? Who was there who would want to bump him off? Or had it been meant for Gorman? A man like him would have many enemies. Well, whichever of them the killer had been after he'd landed him in a nice spot. Here he was with a dead prison guard on his hands — they'd be bound to say he had killed him. There was nothing to be done but to get away before the body was found.

Quickly and methodically he went

through Gorman's pockets, removing what remained of the charred bills and any papers that might lead to identification. After taking the precaution of a hasty look around, he sauntered back into the flare-lit street.

The noise of singing and shouting still came from the saloon and for a moment Glenister contemplated going back with the idea of making his presence seen and so creating an alibi. But he decided against this — the killer might be there and the poker players might recognize him as the man who had called Gorman to follow him outside. His best plan would be to get away from the site of the killing and, if needs be, to return at a later hour, maybe just before the train was due to pull out. One thing was certain — he had to leave town pronto.

3

With this idea in his mind he made his way back to the railroad depot. The construction train might be safe enough for him to make a get-away, but Finney would know that arrangements had been made for him to travel on it, and Gorman was in Finney's pay, could he rely on the latter not to talk?

If he were not on the train there would be no clue to his whereabouts, but his failure to keep his word might suggest that he had ducked out after killing Gorman. Whichever plan he adopted there was the chance of doing the wrong thing. Still, come what may, the open range was his best bet.

The railroad agent greeted him as he pushed open the door. 'Howdy. Yer back in good time for the construction freight.'

'I've bin thinking about that. Ain't

there any other way o' getting to this 'ere Keedie but by that train?'

'Shore is, if yer got the coin to buy a ticket. There's one on the sidings right now pulls out in twenty minutes, and what's more, the big boss's own private car'll be on that train, so yer can figger on the engineer keepin' her rolling.'

'Who's this 'ere big boss yer talk about?'

'What! Yer nary heard o' Theodore Broomfield? He's the fella what aims to build him a railroad right across the High Sierras down into Sacramento Valley and then on to the West coast. You cowhands shore don't keep pace with the times. Why, every news sheet been full of it fer months.'

'When yer range-riding yer don't get much chance o' reading a news sheet. It's only when yer hit town yer hear what the other fellas are doin'. Where is this place Keedie? I were raised in them parts and I never heard of it before.'

'Shore yer ain't. It's named after a plumb good engineer. Take it from me, young fella, a lot's goin' to be heard about Keedie with the C.P. and the W.P. makin' it their headquarters. The way them two outfits love one another the fur's shore goin' ter fly. I reckon that's why Broomfield, who's one of the W.P. bosses, is goin' up there.'

'D'yer reckon a fella could get work up there?'

'Any amount of it. They're cuttin' one another's throats ter get any sort o' workers.'

'I reckon I'll take a look at the place. How much is a ticket goin' ter cost me?'

'Twelve bucks twenty-two. And one day fella, yer goin' to thank me fer sellin' it ter yer.'

'Here's thirteen dollars. Keep the change fer lookin' after my outfit.'

'Thankee. There she blows — she'll be in in a minute and yer'll be in Keedie by midday termorrow. When yer go with one of these construction trains yer nary know when yer goin' ter get there. They gotta stop and pick up stuff at no end o' places. So long, fella, and good luck.'

Glenister lugged his gear on to the side of the track and lit a cigarette. He hoped the agent would remember their confab in case anyone tried to check on his movements.

By the time the train pulled in quite a few travellers had assembled on the depot sidewalk. She was not a big train as trains went — three day cars, a baggage car and, next to the engine the special car for the Big Shot.

This special car was a swell affair with drawn curtains and fancy lights; a negro attendant in a white coat stood at the door.

Glen heaved his saddle and bed-roll into the last car and climbed aboard. He selected a seat with his back to the baggage car and watched his fellow passengers arrive, but he kept one eye on the sidewalk outside in case of trouble.

Slowly, very slowly, the minutes ticked by. Would she never start? From his seat he could see the station agent's clock. He watched the hands as they neared the time of departure.

At last it was time to pull out and the conductor was climbing aboard — there was a sudden shout from the agent. Glen held his breath. Had they discovered the body — were they on his tracks? He was getting ready to make a bolt for it when he saw the reason for the commotion. A woman in a huge hat, the like of which he'd never seen before, bustled up. She was followed by half a dozen fancy-vested gents who'd come to see her off. They were laden with boxes and cases as farewell presents — she shore seemed a popular figure. The party had barely time to say farewell when, at last, the train was under way.

With a sigh of relief, Glenister relaxed and began to take stock of his companions. A man opposite looked like a Jewish drummer, the one sitting next to him was obviously a miner. The most noticeable thing about him was his flaring red shirt.

The lady with the hat (as Glen described her to himself) was further down the car on the opposite side. The conductor seemed to know her — he was making a great fuss to ensure her comfort.

Glen thought the cushions he produced were entirely unnecessary — nature had provided her with ample covering. Her hat fascinated him — it was a marvellous creation covered with scarlet ostrich feathers which any Navajo chief would have given many ponies to possess.

As she raised her hands to remove this work of art, diamonds glittered on every finger. In a low husky voice which he found rather pleasing, she announced to the company that she was 'Railroad Annie', owner of the Line End Saloon in Keedie. Taking a hearty swig from a black bottle which she produced from a carpet bag, she then offered its hospitality to a man sitting near who looked like a Mormon Elder.

Her generous offer was coldly refused. Unabashed, she offered the bottle to a man sitting across the gangway who, apparently, had no qualms in imbibing.

'That's better,' announced Railroad Annie. 'I shore believe in being fortified when I travels.'

A few more 'fortifiers' and the good lady dropped off to sleep. Her snores were loud and regular — she was utterly at peace, oblivious to the bumping and rattling of the train, in a world of her own dreams.

One by one the other passengers stretched themselves out as best they could in their cramped quarters and dozed.

But not Glen. This was his first night of freedom and he wondered how long that freedom would last. Gorman's death had been a jolt to all his plans. If he were picked up now, the guns in his duffle bag would be enough to send him back to the pen. Who would want to kill him? None of the old crowd knew of his release. It must have been someone who had it in for Gorman. There must be hundreds of men whom he had beaten up in his role as prison guard.

There was one thing about his death — poor old Luny would get a bit of peace. His thoughts rambled on till a lurch of the train brought him back to the present. The engineer was shore pushing the old loco along — she was really rolling.

He got up from his seat and stepping over the outstretched legs of the miner, made his way to the observation platform. The cool night air fanned his face, bringing with it the smell of the sage.

Overhead a myriad stars twinkled like gleaming jewels on a black velvet cushion. The rhythm of the wheels and an occasional snort from the engine ahead were the only sounds breaking the silence of the night.

He half sat on the guard rail and watched mile after mile slip by. The coming of the railroads was shore a big thing for the West, but he could never see them taking the place of the horse. Trains must have lines to run on and he knew places where lines could never go. Thinking of horses reminded him that he must get one at the earliest opportunity. He stubbed out his cigarette and returned to his seat.

He must have fallen asleep, for the next thing he knew was that he had been thrown forward by the sudden application of the brakes and was lying on top of the Jewish drummer.

The train was slowing down and he picked himself up and regained his seat. It was still dark outside though the first streaks of grey appearing in the east showed that sun-up was not far away.

He pulled out the makings from his pocket and leisurely rolled a cigarette. As he lit it and leaned back the door of the car was thrown open and a masked man stepped in.

'Sorry to disturb yer shut-eye, folks. Hoist yer hands and keep 'em hoisted and none o' yer won't get hurt. This is a hold-up. Come in, fella,' he called over his shoulder. 'I'm shore there's none of 'em won't oblige by shellin' out to keep our wives and kids from starvin'.'

Another masked man carrying a gunny sack, already well filled, came into the car.

'This is an outrage,' shouted the Mormon-like preacher.

'I ain't figgerin' on gettin' much out of a lantern-jawed critter like you,' said the first bandit. 'But shell out what yer got — pronto.'

The trembling man produced quite a sizeable roll of bills and, after a little further persuasion with the gun, a gold watch.

The bandit then turned his attention to Railroad Annie. Her cursing as she handed over her diamond rings would have made a mule skinner blush. One by one the others parted with their valuables.

Glen sat unmoved awaiting his turn. If he was relieved of his roll the chance of his getting a horse had gone and with it his chance of escape if they were on his trail. He had to do something.

As the masked man who was carrying the sack approached him Glen saw him start. For a moment he seemed so surprised that the gun in his hand wavered.

It was the chance Glen had been waiting for — small enough, but he had to take it. He flicked his burning cigarette straight at the man's eyes, and as he jerked and shook his head, Glen struck with all the power of his muscular shoulders. The bandit dropped like a pole-axed steer and Glen took a headlong dive after his falling gun. The second bandit fired from his place in the doorway — the bullet thudded into the casing behind Glen.

His fingers clawed frantically for the barrel of the fallen gun — another bullet whizzed past his head and found a target in the upholstery of the seat — Glen's fingers found the trigger and for a second the roar of gunfire was terrific.

Somehow the man in the doorway put bullets everywhere around Glenister but not into him, and his fourth shot appeared to strike the man in the shoulder.

Glen ducked for cover — bullets from outside spattered the car's windows and in the half-light of the coming dawn, he caught a glimpse of galloping riders.

The train was now gathering speed and gradually they began to draw away from the robbers while rifle fire from the baggage car caused them to scatter.

Glen picked himself up from the gangway where he had dived for cover from the hail of lead. The other passengers began to reappear; all except the drummer and the Mormon-like preacher, who stayed huddled under the seats.

Railroad Annie 'fortified' herself with a drink from the black bottle and asked in her husky voice, 'Are yer all right, cowboy?' But she received no reply.

Gun in hand, Glenister was half-way

through the car door in pursuit of the bandit whom he hoped he had winged, but he seemed to have made good his escape.

The man Glen had felled was beginning to stir. Glen ripped the mask from his face — he had never seen the galoot in his life. The gunny sack lay where it had been dropped. Glen reloaded his gun from the unconscious man's gunbelt.

'The thieving buzzards,' raved Annie. 'I reckon, stranger, we all owe yer a mighty lot.'

'Nary a thing, marm. This galoot was after my coin the same as yourn.' As he spoke he secured the man's arms with his belt.

The lantern-jawed preacher had now made his appearance — he grabbed for the gunny sack containing the loot.

'Leave that alone, fella. There's mor'n yourn in there and I reckon its the conductor's job to return it to the rightful owners.'

'Yep, that's right,' snapped Annie.

'There's a heap o' my sparklers in there, but what the cowboy says suits me. Where is this blamed conductor, anyway?'

The car door was flung open and a brakeman carrying a rifle appeared.

'About time, too,' shouted Annie. 'When it's all over you show up. A fine railroad this is!'

The brakeman took one look at the bound man and the sack in Glen's hand.

'I reckon it were you, fella, that dun the shooting?'

'Shore was,' said Annie. 'I'm figgerin' it's thanks to him and not to the likes of you, we ain't lost all our possessions. And you're paid to do the job!'

'Will yer keep an eye on this 'ere tied-up fella till I kin locate the conductor?' the brakeman asked Glen.

'Shore. Go right ahead.'

The train was slowing down again and anxiety showed in the passengers' eyes — was it another hold-up? The Jewish drummer glanced out of a window — it was no hold-up this time but the engineer and the train crew coming down the track and folk from the other cars were alighting or poking their heads out of the windows. The prisoner was regaining consciousness, he looked round in a bewildered way and his eyes rested on Glen.

'Hi, there, Roy,' he began, and stopped suddenly.

The name Roy had been a shock to Glen — had anyone else heard it? The only person near enough to have done so was Annie, but she did not appear to have heard.

'I reckon it ain't yer lucky day, fella,' he replied to the bandit. 'But I don't take kindly to losing my coin. 'Specially when it's all I got in the world.'

The eyes of the youngster never left Glen's face, but any further conversation was cut short by the arrival of the train crew. The brakeman indicated Glen. 'This is the fella we gotta thank.'

'Shore is,' chipped in Annie. 'And he

ain't wearing a gun like some others I see around.'

Glen handed over the gunny sack to the conductor.

'I reckon yer'd better take over the loot. Folks will be wantin' their belongings back.'

'You bet we do,' agreed the irrepressible Annie. 'And yer can start right now, Charlie, by diggin' out my sparklers.'

'And my money and my watch,' demanded the Mormon.

'Ladies before hogs,' snapped Annie, who had taken a dislike to her neighbour and could not forgive him for refusing her offer of a 'fortifier'.

'What happened?' Glen asked the engineer.

'They must 'a got aboard when we checked to make the gradient at the bend. The first thing I knowed was when a fella stuck a gun in ma back and told me ter stop. I jerked the emergency brake purty hard in the hope it'd throw him off his balance, but it didn't work. Then he ordered me to keep her moving slowly and I done it till I heered the gun-fire. He hopped out after threatening to plug me if I opened the throttle, but as soon as he wore clear I opened her up. So this is the one yer grabbed — where I dun see him before? I get it — he's boy McCreedie o' the Harper gang. I seed him when they stuck the agent up at Twin Fork Junction. They got away with eight thousand dollars.'

Glen felt as if a bucket of cold water had been poured over him and then he began to sweat. He'd guessed it when he'd heard the name Roy.

'What yer aim to do with him?' asked the engineer.

'I reckon we'd better stop at Twin Fork and the agent kin telegraph back for the sheriff. If we takes him along with us to Keedie he'll be over the State line and into California and we may have to tote him back again. Besides, I reckon the agent'll be right pleased to see 'im. He's been as pesky as a sore hound dog with ticks ever since that hold-up.'

'Right yer are. I'll get her rolling and I'll stop at Twin Forks.'

He and the fireman went back down the train and very soon, with a clanking and groaning the wheels started turning and they were quickly making up their lost time.

Glen left the conductor to return the looted property and again made his way to the observation car. He wanted to be alone to think. He had had a big shock.

4

He found a seat and resting his spurred heels on the rail, he pulled his hat over his eyes and tried to think.

What had he done this time? When he had heard the name Roy, he knew that again he had been mistaken for his younger brother and this time, of all people, by a relation. The boy must be his cousin — one of Uncle Charlie's youngsters. The last time he had seen him he'd been a barefooted brat playing in the muck outside a cabin up in the High Sierras.

Holy Smoke! Then it must be her kid brother — they'd say he'd dropped the kid out of revenge. How it all came back to him. How many times in the loneliness of his prison cell he had seen her with her green eyes and the grace and beauty of a black cougar. Beauty that turned men's heads and caused brothers to hate one another. She was as wicked as she was beautiful and as merciless as a cat with a mouse. Men were like mice to her — she played with them as long as they amused her — played one off against another.

He had been crazy about her from the time she had come to stay with his mother's cousin. So had his brother Roy. And in him she had seen the easy-going, weak-willed son of the outlaw, who loved to spend money — money he had stolen at the point of a gun.

She encouraged him to squander it on expensive presents and when it was gone she would help him plan his next hold-up.

In Glenister she had seen the spoiler of her plans. The elder brother who hated the very sound of the owlhoot. Who'd hated it all his life as he had been dragged by his father from one hide-out to another, until finally the law had caught up with him and he had died with his boots on cursing that same law.

This had been their early upbringing and now Roy, who'd never needed any encouragement to follow in his father's footsteps, had found in her a willing ally.

Glenister ground his teeth as he thought how she had played him for a fool. She had cajoled him to go for a ride with her, to get him out of the way, on the day Roy had robbed the bank. He could see it all now — she had mixed up their shirts so that Roy had worn his sombre coloured ones in place of the gaudy ones he usually sported — no wonder he'd been identified as one of the bank raiders.

Had she come forward at his trial to say that he was with her on the day of the hold-up? No. What was there left for him to do, after his promise to his dying mother that he would look after Roy?

He had done the only thing he could — he had kept quiet and taken the consequences, believing Roy's promise that he would make a fresh start and give up the outlaw life.

Even now he could see them as they sat together in the court when the judge had sentenced him to ten years in the pen.

Not once in the three years he had spent there had he heard a word from them, and now to discover that Roy and her kid brother were members of the Harper gang! One of the worst gangs of desperadoes in the West.

Even in prison their doings had been a topic of conversation. They were 'wanted' in three States and each of them had a price on his head.

The irony of it all — that they should pick on the very train on which he was making his own getaway and that it should be he of all people who had to knock the kid cold.

No wonder Finney had wanted to hire his guns — Roy's identity must be known and one McCreedie was as good as another to a skunk of his calibre.

He failed to see how he could help this kid cousin of his now. His escape was out of the question, and even if he did take a hand he would only be endangering his own neck. No. Promise to his mother or no promise, he was determined that this time Roy had made his own bed and he must lie on it.

His thoughts were interrupted by a pleasant voice saying, 'Good morning.' He pushed his hat off his forehead and looked up to encounter a pair of the bluest eyes he had ever seen.

A tall elegant young woman of about twenty-five was standing in front of him. She was wearing a peach-coloured gown and a large hat of the same shade tied under her chin with a large bow. Her skin reminded him of cream and roses, her nose was small and slightly tip-tilted, her mouth was sweet and gentle-looking, in sharp contrast to her square-cut chin. The face of a gentlewoman who could also be very determined if occasion offered.

'I said, 'Good Morning'. Perhaps it is a little unconventional to address a stranger, but I believe I'm speaking to the hero of last night's hold-up. The conductor told me I should find him here.'

'Howdy, marm. I ain't seed no heroes around whilst I been out here.' Glenister felt irritated — this was obviously one of those Eastern society dames. A member of the society that had sent him to the pen, made his father an outlaw and his brother an outlaw. With what he'd got on his mind right now, he was in no mood to answer fool questions from a gal of her sort.

She laughed. 'I refuse to be put off and I wish to thank you for saving my jewellery. And my father wishes to thank you, too. 'Specially for saving some very valuable documents. We both think your action was very courageous. My father would have come to find you himself, but unfortunately he is suffering from an attack of mountain fever. He'd be pleased if you'd visit him in his car, where he could thank you much better than I.'

'I reckon yer got me wrong, marm. There weren't nort very courageous about last night's fracas. I was only interested in savin' my own coin and didn't give a darn about yer jewellery or yer paw's documents. So I don't reckon I needs his or your thanks. Folks like you would be a lot better off if yer stayed East. Yer see, we ain't civilized out here.'

'I see,' she said quietly. 'I think, sir, you are one of the rudest men I have ever met. And it would perhaps be better for you if you went East — you might learn some manners. Good morning.' With that she turned and left the observation car.

Glen watched her as she walked off the platform. 'Doggorn it,' he muttered to himself, 'I reckon I asked fer that. She's shore some filly — blue grass country ain't in it.'

The train was now well on its way to the High Sierras. The jagged white-capped mountains stood out along the skyline. The Spanish explorers who had named them had done it aptly — razor-toothed was the right description. Below the snowline the forests of firs looked almost black against the whiteness. These in turn gave way to piñons and lower still the creosote and juniper bushes provided a happy hunting ground for the cotton tails who scampered in and out, dodging and hiding from the grey foxes. On the higher slopes grizzlies would be bee-lining and turning old logs over in search of grubs and in the rocks cougar and mountain lion would be hunting the deer.

How he had missed these things — a cool stream teeming with rainbow trout — a silent lake with wild duck streaking out against the evening sky. He watched a jack rabbit as it scampered away from the groaning locomotive. In the distance he saw a bunch of cows — it looked a good year for calves. Who would live in a city when he could live out here? Life was hard and tough — but it was life, real life, and only the fittest survived.

He was still dreaming when the husky voice of Railroad Annie broke through his reverie.

'Hi, cowboy. I guess I ain't thanked yer fer savin' my sparklers. How yer fixed fer coin? I nary met any range hands that weren't flat broke a coupla days after pay day.'

'That's mighty generous o' yer, marm. But it was because I were determined ter keep my coin that I went fer the critter. I gotta get a bronc when I get ter Keedie and I'm figgerin' a good 'un will run purty high with the railroad construction goin' on in those parts.'

'Nary let that worry yer, fella. Annie don't ferget her friends. Just find the bronc that suits yer and tell me the price. It'll be a pleasure. And if there's ort else I can do — say it. I done a lot o' things I ain't proud of in ma time, but I worked hard and them jewels took nigh on thirty thousand o' my earnings. It would have been just too bad if that galoot had made off with 'em. Poor critter — he's only a kid. I figger he knows yer. I ain't fer prying into any fella's business 'cos I don't take kindly to anyone prying into mine, but if yer dodging the law — say so. Railroad Annie knows a hell of a lot mor'n she tells and she's got friends in a lot o' places. So don't ferget, fella, if there's ort I kin do the Line End Saloon will always find me.'

'Thanks, marm, fer yer offer. I shore appreciate it and if there comes a time when I want yer help, I'll be mighty proud to call on yer.'

The corrugated roofs and frame shacks of Twin Fork Junction lay ahead. The small cluster of buildings had been run up to accommodate the station agent and telegraph operator and their families. A loop line had been run into the Junction for the loading of cattle — thus saving the cowmen hundreds of miles of trail driving.

From here they could ship direct to Salt Lake City — thence to Promotion and then to the Union and the big markets of the East. The railroad was opening up the West at a rate which left Glenister spellbound. The long steel rails were taking folks and freight in a matter of days, where previously the journey had taken months.

The train came to a halt with a great jolt. The high smokestack sent up a huge cloud of black vapour which drifted across the sky like a black omen of ill-fortune.

Glenister saw Boy McCreedie hustled down on to the track by the brakeman and the conductor, but he did not move or make any sign.

As he was hustled past the observation platform, the boy looked up at him and spoke for the second time.

'I reckon you and me'll meet again some time, fella, and mebbe it'll be my turn ter holler.'

The brakeman gave him a shove in the back. 'Get a move on. The only hollerin' yer likely ter be doin' will be in the pen.'

Glen watched them until they disappeared into the agent's shack. Then he
took out the kid's gun which he'd
shoved into the top of his jeans and
examined it.

A couple of notches on the butt
interested him — surely they were not
tallies for killings at his age? In spite of
his youth he had the eyes of a killer and
if he had the same blood in his veins as
his sister, he would be capable of
anything.

Glenister had not forgotten his own
plight — there was the telegraph here
and if Gorman's body had been found
— who could tell? In a couple more
hours they would be over the border into
California and he would be safe — there
he could thumb his nose at the law.

His anxiety did not last long — he
saw the conductor and the brakeman
returning from the agent's shack. They
were laughing and appeared pleased
with life and themselves — obviously
there had been no disturbing news sent
over the wire.

In just under three hours they pulled into Keedie — here was the end of the line for passenger traffic. Onwards lay only the construction track into the Feather River country.

As Glen heaved his gear off the car the Jewish drummer came towards him and stuck out his fat podgy hand.

'Thanks, mister, for what yer done. Yer saved me a lot o' dollars and I'm a poor man.'

'Yer welcome, stranger. It were nort.' He took the proffered hand in his steel-like grip. The man winced, but said nothing and hurried away. Glen realized he had a piece of paper in his hand — it was a hundred-dollar bill.

'Well I'll be darned,' he muttered as he pushed it away with his other meagre fortune.

Railroad Annie bustled out of the car with all her boxes and bundles, calling to him not to forget the Line End Saloon. The train crew made a date with him to meet them that night for a drink.

All Glenister really wanted to do was to fade out of the picture but he felt it would be churlish to refuse such generously offered hospitality.

Keedie was larger than the usual construction town. It was a feed and distributing centre for the two great railroad companies.

The Western Pacific and the old Central Pacific both aimed at one thing — to take their lines over the High Sierras and to meet up with the Western railroads. The Western Pacific aimed to join the Denver and Rio Grande and the Central Pacific, the Southern Pacific. Both planned to enter California through the Sacramento Valley. For this reason Keedie had become a boom town. Men of all nationalities mingled on the sidewalks — whites, browns and Chinese jostled each other in a continuous stream.

Sea captains, using the Golden Gate, found lucrative business in bringing the yellow race to work for the construction

contractors, some of the more unscrupulous of whom chartered vessels to
import this cheap labour.

The Chinese were lured over in their
thousands by the promise of much gold
and wealth when their time of service
had expired. Knowing neither the
language nor the customs of a foreign
country, many of them fell easy prey to
the lawless elements of the West.

The white emigrants, mostly Irish
and Swedes, were often the dupes of
slick shysters and 'real estate' men.
They had never earned such money
before in their lives and many found
that they had parted with money
earned by back-breaking months of toil,
for land which did not exist or for
barren rock miles away from the nearest
water.

Every pay day the workers poured
into the town craving for liquor,
gambling and excitement, the company
of women, anything to break the
monotony of their toil with pick, shovel
and sledge.

The riff-raff were waiting for them ready to provide every known form of vice. Honky-tonks, dance halls with their painted harpies, gambling houses with games of monte, poker, blackjack, roulette, faro and dice, abounded. Tinhorn gamblers were everywhere.

Gunfights were an hourly occurrence and it was seldom the town did not claim a dead man for breakfast. The busiest men in Keedie were the undertaker and the sawbones — the one planting and the other saving them.

The railroad was sure bringing prosperity to the West, but it was also bringing the scum.

Glenister found a room in McSweeny's Rest House, which he had to share with four other men, but he felt he was lucky to find even a shake-down.

One night, however, was enough for him — McSweeny's bugs were famous and unless a man was dead drunk and oblivious to bites, he got no rest. He had not been far short of drunk himself.

The hospitality at Railroad Annie's had been fast and furious and a severe test for anyone who had not tasted liquor for a long time.

Among the many folks to whom he had been introduced (and he could not remember half of them) one stood out clearly in his mind — a rancher who was shipping horses to the army at Fort Douglas. He had arranged to meet this man and he hoped to find a mount that would suit him among the bunch.

5

The next morning Glenister was glad to get out of his bug-infested room. He made his way to the shipping pen and climbed on to the top rail to inspect the horses.

He was disappointed. They were a mixed lot — not a really good-looking animal among them. If this was a sample of the future mounts of the 'boys in blue' he was not impressed. They were just a bunch of wild broomtails and if there was a sale for the likes of these it was obvious that he'd have to pay a high price for the good mount he required. Still he had to have a horse, come what may.

He was studying a sorrel mare — he didn't really like her. Her hocks turned in and she had a bad head, short and narrow, but she had a good pair of shoulders on her and looked as if she might have endurance if not speed.

A commotion by a loading shute suddenly drew his attention — four men were trying to force a blindfolded iron grey into a box car.

The horse's unusual markings made Glenister give closer attention to the animal. This was something different — here was a horse, but obviously a bad one to judge from his antics. His iron grey coat was rough, the white tail and mane spoke of palimo blood and had he been chestnut or chocolate brown, he could well have been the mount of some Mexican caballero.

He was not big as horses go, perhaps about sixteen two, but what he lacked in size he made up in other ways. Deep chested, short backed, with a nice neck and a pair of shoulders and hind quarters that shouted power. He was well muscled up, clean limbed with good bone. His flashing hoofs were an off-cream colour giving him a magnificent appearance.

With flaring nostrils and foam-lathered mouth he screamed with rage as the men tried, with blow after blow, to get him to move. Two of them had ropes on either side of him and two others were behind. In spite of all this he bucked and kicked with such ferocity that time and time again the men with the ropes were almost dragged from their feet. Suddenly, with a tremendous bound he reared high in the air and his creamy white hoofs flashed in the morning sunlight with the rapidity of lightning. It was as if he were pounding a silent and unseen drum. At that moment a construction loco whistled as it pulled out and the sudden strange noise seemed to send the blindfolded creature into an even worse temper or panic. Again he rose high into the air — the man with the rope on the near side was jerked completely off the ground.

Natural battler as this stallion was, he sensed his chance, whipped round at the second man and charged him.

It takes a braver man than most to stand in the way of an infuriated wild stallion and the rope handler was no exception — he jumped out of the way.

The great beast was loose, blindfolded and with ropes dangling from his neck. A cry went up from the crowd of spectators who had gathered to watch and many dived for cover.

High up on the top rail of the shipping pen, Glenister, perfectly safe, had a grandstand view and was thoroughly enjoying the scene. His sympathies were all with the horse — man against beast — who would conquer?

Outnumbered by four to one, handicapped by the dangling ropes and what was worse, the blindfold, could this wild creature escape his tormentors and make for the open range and freedom across the tracks?

For a moment he stood and sniffed the air as if sensing the sage-covered slopes. He snorted in defiance and pawed the ground beneath his hoofs.

The locomotive whistled again — the animal trembled from head to foot. What was this strange sound? What new unseen foe had he to face?

The shouting of the crowd increased. The man who had first lost hold of the rope quickly grabbed it again as it trailed in the dust. The stallion either felt or sensed his nearness and bucked madly. Then, as if he had made up his mind, he turned to head in the direction of the railroad building.

A cry, almost a scream, came from the crowd — there, right in the animal's path, toddling along clutching a doll, was a child of about three. Unconcernedly, with golden curls blowing in the breeze, she was coming to see what all the shouting was about — unaware of the danger that faced her.

'Shoot the brute,' yelled a panic-stricken voice.

'My baby, my baby,' came a woman's scream.

A second before Glen had seen the child and was racing straight for the stallion; a desperate idea had come into his head — the memory of a trick he and his brother Roy had practised with their own mounts. But a wild stallion was a very different proposition from a trained cow pony.

The horse had not started to run because of the blindfold and it was for this reason Glen gambled on his desperate action. He knew that if he failed those cream hoofs would trample him beyond recognition or crack his skull like an egg-shell.

As if bulldogging a steer he dived with outstretched hand, not for the neck as in bulldogging, but for the animal's two forelegs.

His aim for the off fore was bang on the target and with a grip like a steel vice he grabbed the bone above the fetlock. His aim with his left arm was a fraction high — he fumbled, but made it and with a mighty heave of his powerful shoulders he jerked the forelegs sideways, threw the stallion off balance and brought him to the ground with a tremendous thud.

His second danger lay in the thrashing hind legs. As he felt the body hit the ground he rolled over out of the way of the flashing hoofs and, with the agility of a cat, scrambled to his feet. Before the surprised grey could regain his feet Glenister's knee was pinning its head to the ground.

A great cheer went up from the crowd. The toddler, with large brown eyes was staring at him from barely six feet away. In a second someone had whisked her away to safety as the range riders gathered round to secure the stallion.

Glen patted the sweating animal's neck. 'It's shore tough on yer, old fella, 'cos I reckon yer wouldn't o' touched that mite if yer'd been able ter see her.'

'That's little yer know, stranger. This critter's a killer,' said one of the rope men.

'Shore is, fella. We know,' added another. 'It's taken us nigh on three months to capture 'im.'

So they were wild horse hunters, were they? 'How much d'yer want fer him?' Glen asked, still keeping the stallion's head down as the men secured a stronger hold on the ropes.

The first man laughed. 'I reckon we owe yer summat, fer it were the purtiest bit o' bulldogging I ever seed; but yer ain't got enough coin ter buy 'im — we aims ter make a fortune out o' that stallion. We're taking 'im down to Cheyenne in Wyoming fer the bucking contest at the Rodeo and from there on to Pendleton and Phoenix. He ain't ever bin rid and I'm bettin' he nary will.'

Glen relinquished his position to one of the other men and stood up. 'When I was a kid my paw used to have a saying — 'There never was a rider that couldn't be throwed, there never was hoss foaled that couldn't be rode.' '

He hated to think of this noble creature being dragged from one Rodeo to another — spurred from shoulder to flank to make him buck. A bad horse was always bad, but there'd come a day when he'd be too old to buck or a heavy fall would put out a shoulder or break a leg and then he'd be for skinner's yard. Mabbe he was a killer, but he'd like to have a try at gentling him.

'I'll give yer five hundred fer him.'

The man sneered. 'Five hundred! Twice that won't buy 'im. I tell yer he's not fer sale.'

'What is his price, man? I'll pay anything in reason.' The question was asked in a cultured Eastern voice by one of the watching crowd. Both rope men turned to see who had spoken. They saw an elderly grey-haired man wearing obviously city clothes and standing by his side was the girl in the peach-coloured frock who had spoken to Glenister on the train.

'I reckon yer dun heard what I said to this fella, mister — he ain't fer sale.'

Into the eyes of the pale, drawn face of the Easterner came the look of a determined man — one not easily to be turned from any project he might have in mind.

'I asked you the price — now I demand it.'

The man sneered again. 'And who might you be that 'demands' things?'

'I am Theodore Broomfield. That horse will not leave on any train owned by my Corporation.'

At the mention of the name Broomfield all eyes turned in his direction. So this was the railroad builder — Glen found himself looking into the blue eyes of the girl — this was the man he had refused to see — the great Broomfield.

Well that was that — he shrugged his shoulders and turned to leave. The wild horse hunter spoke — into his eyes had come a mean cunning look.

'Well, as so many folks seem blamed keen to buy the horse, I'll tell yer what we'll do, fella. I reckon if yer can ride him, 'e's yourn fer five 'undred bucks and I'll lay yer another level 'undred yer can't.'

Glenister hesitated before replying.

He could feel the girl's eyes on him. Had she wanted the horse? It was three years since he'd had a leg over a saddle — had he lost his old skill in those years in Rocky Point? He was asking a big lot of himself to top this brute. He looked up and her eyes met his — in them he could read a challenge.

'It's a go, fella. And yer on ter yer hundred.'

The rancher whom he had met the night before had joined the group. 'Are you aimin' on a ride to a finish, or the standard bronc-buckin' time of ten seconds?' he asked.

The wild horse hunter replied, 'I said ride 'im, and ride 'im I means. And what's more we'll 'ave it in the livery corral. This ain't no Rodeo and what's more we ain't takin' no chances o' 'im getn' loose when he's put this fella in the dust.'

As Glenister turned to leave for the ride he felt a hand on his arm. A woman with tear-filled brown eyes stood at his side, with the golden-haired toddler in her arms. In an Irish brogue you could have cut with a knife, she spoke to him.

'Thank ye, sorr. It's a right brave man that ye are to be shore.'

Glen smiled down at her. 'It were a pleasure, marm.' He pinched the child's rosy cheek. 'Hi yer, Sunshine. Yer weren't ter know he were a wild one, were yer now?'

'Naughty gee-gee,' lisped the little one.

'Shore a naughty gee-gee,' he repeated and touched his hat to the mother.

'Good luck to ye, sorr. If ye ever want a friend, ask for Jim Donovan, the engineer. He'll shore be wantin' to thank ye himself when he hears of what you've done.'

News of the pending ride had travelled fast and by the time Glen had collected his saddle a big crowd had already assembled at the livery corral. Gamblers missed no chance for a wager.

'Five to one he don't ride 'im,' Glen heard one shout.

'Here, I'll lay two to one he takes a dive inside ten seconds.'

'Hey there, Kansas Jack,' came Railroad Annie's husky voice, 'I'll take yer five thousand to a thousand. I seed that cowboy in action and it were when lead was flyin' — nary toppin' a bronc.'

Others in the crowd followed her lead and the betting grew. The grey was led in blindfold. He was fighting mad with fear and the rough handling he was receiving from his captors made him worse. Open-mouthed he tried to get his teeth into anything or anyone that came within his reach. By sheer brute force they snubbed him to the post in the middle of the corral — it was the only way they could get a saddle on him. As Glen heaved it on to his back the animal cringed.

'Yer shore got a fancy saddle,' said the leader of the hunters. 'Yer wouldn't be wantin' ter bet that, too, would yer?'

Glen was far too busy with the cinches to take any heed. Satisfied that it was secure he hitched up his jeans, pulled his hat well on to his head and climbed into the saddle. As he did so he again caught sight of the girl — so she had come. Perhaps it was in hope of seeing this 'rude gentleman' as she had called him, hit the ground. Feet firmly in the stirrups he gave the word: 'Let him go.'

The blindfold was whipped off. For a second the wild red-eyed stallion stared about defiantly. Then he realized that for the first time in his life he had something on his back.

He kicked his hind legs violently into the air — then his head went down and he started to buck. As soon as he felt the first reaction of the powerful muscles, Glen knew he had a fight on his hands — one of them had to be the loser. He had set his mind on having the horse and he wanted to answer the challenge he had seen in the girl's eyes. Up went the grey for the second time, to come down stiff-legged with such force that it jarred him to the bottom of his spine. Time and time again the horse repeated the manœuvre — twisting himself into a jack-knife posture or an inverted U. But Glen was riding easy. In spite of his hatred of steel he clamped his spurs into those heaving flanks: the grey had to be shown that he had found a master.

The shouting of the crowd had become a roar — Glen never heard it, so set was he on the task in front of him.

Finding that bucking did not shift this hated two-legged creature from his back, the stallion commenced to rear until he was standing almost upright. The first rear caught Glenister unawares and so quickly had the horse thrown up his head that it struck him in the face with a blow which almost squashed his nose flat. The claret began to flow — he could feel it warm on his lips.

The sight brought a roar from the crowd. 'Ride him, cowboy. Stick it, fella,' came from all sides.

Glen's head was swimming. The

ground seemed to be dancing up and down as the grey started sunfishing and spinning round like a top in between tremendous rears. Then he began to buck again, but his powerful muscles were beginning to tire.

Glen's head was clearing; he had lost count of time, he only knew that it seemed an age since he began battling with this thing of the wild. His leg muscles and his knees and calves were tiring fast, his grip had not been used for so long.

He ground his teeth, determined to stick it — one of them had to crack sooner or later, and it should not be him.

The grey seemed as equally determined. Suddenly from bucking he gave a tremendous rear, throwing himself completely backward in a violent effort to dislodge his rider.

Glen knew the trick — once he was on the ground the horse would try either to roll on him or savage him. As the animal was falling Glen kicked his feet out of the stirrups and allowed himself to slide backwards till he touched the ground and then stepped quickly to one side. He staggered slightly, for a moment he thought his knees were going to buckle under him, but as the horse rolled over and regained his legs Glen was once more firmly fixed in the saddle with feet in stirrups.

This final effort seemed to discourage the grey — his movements began to flag. It was the moment for which Glen had been waiting. He started to spur from shoulder to flank, it was now that he had to show the stallion who was the master. He hated doing it and devoutly hoped that it would be the last time that he would have to use spurs on such a game battler.

The crowd had gone mad with excitement at the sight of the spurring, but relentlessly Glen continued to spur the foam-lathered, sweat-soaked animal until finally the grey dropped stiff-legged and stood still.

His head went down — his spirit was

broken for the time being, he recognized that the man on top was the master, but he would never know how nearly the victory had been his. Glenister knew that if he dismounted he would fall and there was one more thing left for him to do. 'Drop those rails,' he yelled to the onlookers.

As the rails of the corral clattered to the ground he spurred the grey forward and out on to the rolling sage. The stallion had recovered some of his spirit and finding that he had a chance to run, he bounded away, leaving the roaring, yelling crowd far behind.

Glen thrilled and marvelled at the animal's power. He had ridden many good horses in the past, but none would have come up to this stallion. In spite of the gruelling time he had just gone through, he needed no urging to run. It seemed to Glen that he was running for the sheer joy of running — thankful to be away from the whistling train and shouting people.

Glenister made no attempt to check

or guide him — he was content to let strength gradually creep back into his own aching limbs.

On and on went the grey across the sage grass-covered plateau, past greasewood and scrub. He negotiated gopher holes with the agility of one accustomed to the wilds and its hazards.

The wind blowing on Glen's face brought with it the pungent scent of the sage and the freshness of the mountains. He was back — back in his beloved West with a good horse under him. How many times during his sentence in Rocky Point had he dreamed of such a ride. There it had been only a dream — here was the reality.

They sped across the plateau and soon began to climb the lower slopes of the mountains; the sage gave way to clumps of creosote bushes and juniper thickets. Higher still Glen could see the piñons and cedars, the laurels and, higher still, the forests of firs. On the topmost peaks, where the foot of man had never trod, snow glistened against the clear blue skyline.

The sound of gurgling water and the sight of a crystal stream brought Glenister's thoughts back to earth; he realized that both he and his mount could do with a drink. He put pressure on the reins — gently at first and then more firmly. He had no wish to cause more pain to those lathered, tender jaws. It would take time and much gentle handling before the horse would be accustomed to the steel bit — gentle handling until the sensitive mouth would respond to the lightest touch. There was a lot that the stallion had to be taught before he would be the trained range horse Glenister required. It would take time.

He dismounted stiffly and holding the reins firmly he led the grey towards the water. Though the animal badly wanted to drink, he was still suspicious of the two-legged thing which had been on his back. Twice he stopped and hesitated before sinking his velvety muzzle into the clear cold water.

Glen ran a gentle hand down the arched neck. 'All right, old fella, take it easy. I know well how yer feel,' he said in a soft caressing voice. 'I been a prisoner, too. It's bad, but yer kin get used to it in time. Talking o' prisons, I reckon Rocky'd be a good name fer you.' He put out a hand to touch the horse's muzzle, but Rocky's eyes rolled till most of the whites were showing, his ears went back and his mouth opened showing bared teeth.

'All right if that's how yer feel. But the sooner yer learns I ain't goin' ter hurt yer, the sooner we'll be better friends. I'd like ter let yer roll, but I ain't gotta rope so I reckon it'll have ter wait fer another time. Let's see what we kin do to these flanks o' yourn, when I've taken a drink myself.'

He led the stallion to a stout tree and tied the reins securely. Then he went back to the stream and drank deeply. In the mirror-like water he saw the blood on his face — he removed his bandanna and cleaned himself up.

The water refreshed him, but every bone in his body still ached. Rinsing out his bandanna he hung it on a low branch to dry, then, in spite of his stiffness and aches, he collected bunches of sage grass and set about bathing Rocky's blood-bespattered flanks. It was no easy task, but gradually the animal seemed to sense that this human was trying to help him.

Glenister next removed the saddle and wiped down the sweat-soaked body, then after making sure that the animal was well secured, he stretched himself out in the shade to rest.

It was late in the afternoon and the sun was well down in the west when he wakened. His first thought was for the horse. He was standing with his head up and as Glenister approached he snorted defiantly, but he did not bare his teeth.

Glen picked up the saddle and the horse never took his eyes from it.

'Now this ain't goin' ter hurt yer

none. I gotta have something ter sit on, so don't be so blamed ornery.'

Rocky cringed and kicked out wildly as the saddle touched his back, but the reins held him firm — he was learning fast. As he felt the cinch round his belly he took in great gulps of air in an endeavour to inflate himself, but a knee stuck into him made him relax.

'I wasn't born yesterday, old fella. Come on, Rocky, you and me gotta date in town. That there wild hoss hunter's mebbe thinkin' we done sloped off without payin' him.' As he put his foot into the stirrup he felt the horse's hot breath on his back, but he made no attempt to bite.

The rest had refreshed both man and beast and when Glenister gave the horse its head they literally flew over the ground. The lights were already burning in Keedie when the town came into view.

Glen went on talking in his quiet soothing voice. 'Now for some chuck fer the pair of us. I bet yer've never tasted real oats.'

People on the sidewalks turned to watch as he headed for the livery stable. When they entered the main street Glen found that he sure had his hands full — Rocky certainly hated anything to do with town and folks.

The owner of the livery and two of his hands came out to meet him. They stared in astonishment and their attention was quickly centred on Rocky.

'Yer shore dun it, fella. I take my hat off ter yer.'

'Gotta box stall, mister?' asked Glen.

'No, nary ort like that. But yer welcome to a stall, tho' I figger yer'll never get him through that door.'

'I reckon there's only one thing fer it — it's the snubbin' post till we leave town. Loan me yer strongest halter and bring me the best feed o' oats yer got — and water.'

Having seen Rocky safely secured, fed and watered, Glenister made for the store and grub-staked himself for a trip into the hills.

It was out there in the quiet open country and there alone, that he would be able to gentle Rocky, and he aimed to do that before looking for work. He realized that he was ravenously hungry and now that his most pressing business had been completed, he went off in search of chuck.

6

Glenister turned into the first clean eating-house he saw. A smiling waitress hurried over to take his order. The story of his saving a small child from a wild stallion had spread all over the town and the female population gave him a warm place in their hearts.

The waitress, in particular, felt that she could not do enough for him since she was a relative of Donovan, the child's father. She stood by in admiration as he consumed a huge meal. The rescue of the little girl and his mastery of the bad horse combined to make him a hero in her eyes.

He paid his check and went in search of the wild-horse hunters. He wanted to make sure as quickly as possible that Rocky was really his property.

Finally he ran them to earth in the Line End Saloon. He was given a great reception, men crowded round him and he was the subject of more back-slapping than he had previously endured in the whole of his life.

Railroad Annie, genuinely pleased to see him and more than elated over her win from Kansas Jack, insisted on drinks 'on the house'. Strangers greeted him with such cordiality that he found it overwhelming.

Eventually he managed to buttonhole the leader of the horse hunters. The man's hostile manner had undergone a complete change. He shook Glen warmly by the hand and congratulated him.

Glenister was more than surprised: 'I reckon I owe yer four hundred dollars, fella.'

'That's where yer wrong, mister. It's me that owes yer a hundred bucks. Annie, here, insisted on payin' us fer the hoss out o' her winnin's. Yer shore put up a hell of a ride. Yer wastin' yer time — get yerself down to the Rodeos. A fella that kin ride like you 'ud be in the top money in no time.'

Glenister was dumbfounded to hear of Annie's generosity. He hurried off to find her. 'Yer can't do this,' he began.

'Can't I? I've done it and here's yer bill o' sale fer that man-killer. I only hope he don't break yer neck.' She pushed the bill into his hand. 'There's no need thankin' me — it's yerself I've got ter thank fer winnin' me four thousand five hundred from Kansas Jack. It shore tickled me pink ter take it off him. Besides, I reckon he owes it to me — the years I've let him use my saloons. That fella seems to have been around wherever I been fer nigh on longer than I care ter think about. So come on, all o' yer, belly up — I'm buyin'.'

Glen still felt overwhelmed and tried to find words to express his feelings, but she would have none of it and had he persisted further he would only have succeeded in making the situation uncomfortable for everyone.

The horse hunter paid over the

hundred dollars he had lost and continued to urge him to become a professional bronc rider. In this he was joined by Kansas Jack, who seemed no ways perturbed by losing that much coin to Annie.

Much as Glenister appreciated the hospitality and kindness showered upon him from all sides, he was anxious to make his getaway. Rocky was very much on his mind. He had no intention of leaving the horse snubbed to a post.

He waited his opportunity and as soon as his new found friends were otherwise engaged, he slipped quietly out of the saloon and made his way back to the livery. It would be a long time before Rocky would stand for a pack on his back and a second horse would have to be found.

He had a careful look around and after some time he found a mare which he thought would suit his purpose. She was no picture, but she had good shoulders and was clean-legged. He bought her for a hundred dollars, saddled her and loaded up his packs. Then, leading Rocky on a lariat, he headed for the open country.

He rode through the night and as the moon came up long streaks of silver struck against the sharp saw-edged peaks of the High Sierras. Jet-black shadows were thrown across his path by the sage brush and creosote bushes. Taking his bearing from the North star he rode towards the mountains.

Morning found him camped in a sheltered draw where there was good feed and water for the horses — a short rest and he pushed on for the piñon country. It was there, on the blue grama grass and among the piñons, that he proposed to gentle Rocky, to rub up his gun draw and generally re-accustom himself to life in the wilds.

In a diminutive forest of stunted piñons he selected his permanent camp. The spot he choose was ideal. A crystal clear mountain stream bubbled and gurgled between shallow banks; willows and white trunked cottonwoods fringed its edges. Juniper bushes grew in clumps — their wax-like berries showing like pearls against their dark foliage. The fall is the most beautiful time in the piñon country. The air is laden with the sweet scent of the piñon nuts, their cones, with henna-coloured centres and flaring bunches of brown berries cover the bushes. The piñon jays are to be seen at their best, in their blue plumage.

As Glenister began his preparations for his temporary home, these beautiful birds chattered abuse at the intruder, but the yellow warbler in the willows seemed to sing a song of welcome.

In these surroundings he decided to build his cabin and for the next few days the woods resounded to the sound of his axe. He worked ceaselessly and very soon a pine log cabin was completed and a rough rail corral had been run up for the horses.

Glenister looked round at the result of his labour. He breathed a deep sigh of contentment and thankfulness. A picture of his cell in Rocky Point flashed through his mind and a shudder ran down his spine. Then and now, he thought. Can it be the same world?

Now that his immediate wants were catered for, Glen was free to set about the business of gentling Rocky and perfecting his gun draw. As he slipped the gunbelt around his waist and felt the weight of his guns on his thighs, it was, for him, once more like old times — he felt fully dressed at last.

He tied the thongs of the holster to his legs and practised his draw with either hand. His time in Rocky Point had made him painfully slow — gone was the rapid co-ordination between hand and eye. He broke open a box of shells, took an empty bean can and set it up fifty yards away. With methodical care he loaded his guns — turned his back to the can, swung round on his heel and fired. The can did not move, but the gunfire scared Rocky badly. He tore round the corral screaming with fear.

Glenister cursed quietly and went over to the corral rail. In a soothing voice he began to talk to the terrified animal. 'Yer've got to get used to it, old fella. Gunfire's part of yer education. There's a lot yer gotta get used to. Them there fancy hoofs o' yourn have got to be shod. Now, take a look at this old lady — she ain't in no ways disturbed.'

The mare was grazing contentedly. Glenister held out a hand towards her and she whinnied affectionately.

He went back doggedly to his target practice. He was slow — darn slow, and what was worse he'd lost his accuracy — his uncanny skill which had made his friends marvel and his enemies fear and respect him. He was no seeker of fame as a gunman — he never had been, but he knew that the reputation other folk had built up around him, still lived.

One day a cheap gun slick in search of fame would seek him out and his likeness to his brother Roy constituted another danger. Roy, who was now running with one of the worst gangs in the West.

He must go on practising — he dare not take any chances, he had to be prepared to meet any eventuality that the future might hold in store for him. All he asked of fate was to be left alone to go his own way and live his own life, to forget the lawlessness of his upbringing as a child, to live peaceably with his fellow men, but there was no certainty that his desire would be granted.

Day after day for the next few weeks he continued with the gentling of the stallion and persistent gun practice, until eventually, his patience bore fruit. His old skill returned — he was chain-lightning on the draw and there was little to choose between either hand. He could knock over a running jack rabbit with a rifle at four hundred yards.

Rocky, too, had become a reformed character — up to a point. With the loving care and attention lavished upon him he had lost some of his fear of the human race. He had grown into a magnificent animal; his iron-grey coat shone like burnished steel. The cream hoofs, mane and tail flashed in the sunlight as he carried his now loved master over the open countryside.

He was a fully trained range horse, with no fear of gun or rope. There was no longer need to tether or hobble him — he would follow Glenister around like a dog and would come at his whistle. But he would have no truck with strangers and was not friendly to other horses. He would put up with a mare, but he would turn savagely on a horse or a stranger if they came too near for his liking.

On a warm afternoon of the late Indian summer Glenister sat by the stream fishing for trout. He was not without company; a few yards below him stood old man Pelican. Huge rainbow trout idled beneath the over-hanging banks, or darted through the water with such speed that their brilliant colouring gleamed like jewels through the clear stream. Scarlet-and-blue kingfishers dived and swooped over the foam-flecked water from their home among the willows.

On the bank above Rocky grazed contentedly — a sudden whinny attracted Glen's attention. With head erect, the horse was gazing westward. Glen got up from his seat by the stream and going over to the horse, he looked in the same direction in which the animal was 'pointing'.

In the far distance he could see two riders approaching. He returned to the stream and picked up a five-pounder which he had just landed and, followed by Rocky, headed back for the cabin.

He had left two flat stones on the open camp fire to heat for the preparation of his evening meal and on these stones he placed the fish and a large black coffee-pot. The carcass of a long-eared mule deer and a brace of quail hung from the branch of a near-by cottonwood — a man could live well in the wilds from the prowess of his gun.

The riders drew nearer and as they reached hailing distance Glenister could see that one of them was a woman. He could scarcely believe his eyes — it was the girl of the train — the railroad boss's daughter.

'Doggorn it, Rocky, I'm figgerin' she's tracked yer down and she's still hankerin' after buyin' yer.'

Rocky pawed the ground and snorted, but he did not move.

The second rider was a man of about forty — a big man, dressed like a lumberjack in jeans tucked into high-laced boots. 'Howdy,' he called as they drew rein. 'Yer shore take some findin', fella. It's taken us nigh on a week to locate yer, though we knew yer were in this neck o' the woods somewhere.'

The girl had not spoken, she was looking at Rocky with admiration in her eyes.

'Howdy,' drawled Glen. He was not at all pleased at their arrival.

The girl turned to him and smiled. 'What a wonderful job you've made of the horse. I knew you would — I'm so glad.'

Her obviously sincere praise did much to soothe Glen's feeling of irritation. Inwardly he was flattered and pleased.

'Won't yer lit down and eat?' he asked. 'It'll be only grilled trout and flapjacks and the coffee's on the boil. Yer right welcome.'

'Thank yer, we'd shore like to,' said the man, 'but we've got to be back in Keedie by sundown. I'd better introduce myself — I'm Lyttleton, Assistant Superintendent on the Railroad, and this is the chief's daughter, Miss Elizabeth Broomfield. My chief's been looking fer you since the day you rode yonder noble creature.' He nodded towards Rocky, who was showing signs of his distrust of strangers. 'The chief wants you to call and see him. He has a proposition he wants to put to yer.'

Glenister was squatting over the fire

— he looked up with a half-grilled trout on a stick in his hand.

'If it's about buyin' the hoss I can save myself a journey and you any more time — he's not fer sale.'

Lyttleton looked perplexed. The girl laughed and her voice sounded to Glen like the tinkling of water in a mountain stream.

'My father never wanted the grey. He wanted to buy it for you in recognition of the service you rendered to him in regaining those valuable documents from the train robber.'

'I reckon I must have misunderstood him, marm.'

'I would love to have such a wonderful horse, but I could never ride him. My riding is such that I have to have a docile old beast like this fellow here. Can we tell my father that you'll ride in to see him tomorrow? You'll find him in his car on the sidings.'

Glenister rose to his full height and looked the girl straight in the eyes.

'I can't figger out what yer paw can

want with a fella like me. I know naught about railroads, but I'll be there. I gotta ride in for supplies anyhow.'

'Thank you. Good-bye.'

'So long, fella,' called Lyttleton as they turned their mounts and headed down the draw.

Glen watched them till they were out of view. 'What yer make o' that, Rocky? I reckon I had it all wrong about 'em wanting you. Ain't she just a humdinger of a gal. I'm figgerin' that fella Lyttleton's sweet on her.'

But Rocky was no longer interested — the strangers had gone and he was content to go on cropping the grass.

Glen laughed. 'So that's all the help yer gives me! You wait till yer get yer eye on some mare yer fancies and I'll be just as helpful.'

The next morning he rode into Keedie and ground-reined Rocky outside Broomfield's special car. He knocked on the door, which was opened by a clerkish individual wearing a cutaway coat and a high white collar.

At the man's invitation he stepped inside.

As Glenister entered, the railroad boss glanced up from a large table strewn with papers — mostly maps — at which he had been working. 'Ah, you. So you've actually shown up at last. Take a seat.' He pointed to a chair on the opposite side of the table. 'I'm afraid I don't know your name.'

For a moment Glenister hesitated. 'Glenister — John Glenister.'

'You know mine, it's Broomfield. Well, Glenister, I asked you to call here to offer you a job. I've had proof of your courage on three separate occasions and your active, resourceful brain and pugnacity under adverse conditions. I want men with those qualities around me — I want you. I am prepared to pay your own price — in moderation of course. I suggest you start at five hundred a month. All I ask in return is your absolute loyalty.'

Five hundred dollars a month — it almost took Glen's breath away. What would he have to do for that money?

'It's a mighty lot of coin yer offering, Broomfield, but I knows naught about railroad building. If it's my guns yer buying — they ain't fer sale.'

A look which had made big bankers quail came into Broomfield's eyes; but it had no such effect upon Glenister.

'Young man, there is more in building a railroad than the actual railroad itself. As for your guns — here beyond the laws of common civilization, undoubtedly they'll be of use. But it's your courage I want and your knowledge of the country and the folk who live here. In this job it's the smaller things that present the greatest difficulties. There's local prejudice against the railroad, and one of the difficulties is to provide food for the workers.

'The lawless element must be suppressed and agitators amongst the workers got rid of. New work teams have to be hired. At present all these are losing me time — time means money and the loss of money will mean the loss of the railroad. Bankers and stockholders are only interested in results and low costs. I want results. If I get results, low costs will follow.

'Discontent is rife among the workers and a great deal of it can be put down to the difficulty of getting fresh beef. Ostensibly your job is to keep the camp supplied with meat. At the same time I want you to keep your ears open and see if you can find the reason that so many workers are quitting. I've always given preference to white men, but if things don't change I shall have to take on Chinese like my competitors.'

Broomfield got up from his chair, walked over to the car window and pointed to the High Sierras. 'Those mountains are, in themselves, a formidable task to conquer. Just a great mass of granite. They've defeated others who had the same idea as I have, but they're not going to defeat me. My only route is down the valley of the Feather River.

'The Oroville and Virginia City folk

were beaten when they tried to go by the north fork and the Central Pacific in the east. So I am left with the west fork and the railroad's going through there by way of the Beckworth Pass.

'The Central's going through American River Canyon and aims to cross at Donner Pass. It's going to be a race — one of the greatest in American railroad history.

'And the Central, with the Southern Pacific behind them, have resources which we have not. Now do you understand why I want men with courage and ability with me? The task will be a hard one, so it's up to you.'

Glenister had listened with interest to all Broomfield had to say. The job offered possibilities and a certain amount of excitement. He saw railroad building in a new light.

'If yer want me with yer, I'm yer man.'

'Good. That's what I hoped you'd say.' The big shot turned from the window, and as he did so he caught sight of Rocky. 'Surely that's the wild stallion?'

'Shore is.'

'A man that can do that with a horse is all right by me. Go over and see Lyttleton, the Assistant Superintendent. He'll put you wise to the general run of things. He's a good man, but not used to this wild country. Remember, Glenister, I'm behind you in everything. Don't let me down.'

They shook hands; it was the sealing of a bond — a bond based on the judgment of one man.

Outside Glenister found a man waiting for him. A big man in blue jeans and wearing the traditional peaked cap of an engineer. He came forward with outstretched hand.

'I'm right proud to meet yer, sir. The wife saw yer ride up. I'm the pappy of the little girl yon hoss nigh did for.'

Glen took the proffered hand and grinned. 'It was nary as bad as that. I figger Rocky didn't know she wore there. Yer see, they had him blindfolded.'

'Just the same, if ever I kin do yer a favour, all yer gotta do is name it. Or Jim Donovan is not my name.'

'That's shore mighty good of yer, Jim, and I don't forget it. Glenister's the name. My friends call me Glen.'

'O.K., Glen. The wife'd be mighty proud if yer'd step in and take a bite o' grub with us.'

'I'd be honoured to. I gotta get to know you railroad folks — I'm going to be one of yer. But I must see to my hoss first. I just agreed to work for the big boss in yonder and right now I gotta find me this fellow Lyttleton.'

'Yer'll find him in the last shack but one. I just seed him go in.'

7

Glenister pushed open the door of the shack. Lyttleton was poring over a pile of papers.

'Hello there. So yer arrived. Sit down and I'll take yer over to see the Chief in a coupla minutes.'

'I dun seed him. I agreed to join the payroll as beef chaser.'

'Thank the lord for that. Gettin' beef fer that mob's almost sent me round the bend. I'm an engineer — not a commissary o' stores, and I guess these beef contractors must think I'm the biggest sucker outta New York, judging on the toughness o' the cows they palmed on to me lately.'

Glen laughed; he liked this fellow's frankness. 'The Chief, as yer calls him, said you might put me wise as to what this here job is. I'm a plumb greenhorn on railroads.'

'Well, briefly we aims to build a railroad over the High Sierras down Feather River Valley into the Sacramento Valley and on to Pueblo. We're split into two sections — the one from Pueblo and us from the Nevada line. It hasn't been too bad till we hit these High Sierras, but those doggorn mountains are naught but solid granite. The deep canyons and gulches are enough to break the heart of the toughest railroad engineer in the world. But not Theodore Broomfield's, even though he is a sick man. It wouldn't be so bad if the contract didn't call for a one per cent gradient and no more than ten-degree curves. In this mountainous country, it's almost impossible. It ain't even fair, for our rivals can get away with a two-and-a-half per cent gradient.'

Though Glen had only the faintest idea what the engineer was talking about, he agreed. Perhaps if he listened to a little more, he'd begin to understand.

Lyttleton went on with his story: 'You see, the Central Pacific have got the Southern Pacific behind them and the American River Canyon's easy working. But the old man's got 'em beat — he's building on the west side of the mountains. That means we'll get all the sun.'

This made no light on Glen. 'What's the sun gotta do with building railroads?' he blurted out.

Lyttleton laughed. 'I was forgetting yer ain't a railroad man. Yer see, the sun will melt the snow sooner on the west side, and I'm guessing I've no need to tell yer what the snow can be like in the winter.'

It was Glen's turn to grin. 'I reckon not. I mind the time when twenty-foot drifts were naught. For the life of me I can't figger on how you fellas aim to work when the snow's around. Folk up there just see to the stock and stick around the stoves indoors in winter.'

Lyttleton sighed. 'I guess we'll have to do the same. The only consolation we'll have is that the C.P. will be in the same boat. It's shore hell on the workers in that weather and the biggest headache's feeding 'em. Flour, sugar, coffee and such-like don't worry us none, the freight cars can haul that in, but it's fresh meat that's the trouble, and that's why the boss was determined to get a man he could trust, who knew cattle. That's why he picked on you. I reckon Miss Elizabeth had a lot to do with it. It was her mentioned you to her father, and the way you'd handled the train robbers and that wild hoss o' yourn, convinced him.'

Glenister was flabbergasted. 'Yer mean, yer mean,' he stammered, 'it wore her that dun this?'

'I certainly do. And I'm thinking she's shore handed yer a tough assignment as they'd say back home. Well, tomorrow we'll leave for the camp. The construction train leaves here about eleven.'

'Thanks, but I'll ride over and meet yer there if yer don't mind. I'm figgering Rocky ain't used to yer locomotives yet.'

'Just as yer like. But I want yer to meet the Superintendent. Yer'll like him — he's a great guy, is Grainger, and as tough as they come.'

'Where's this camp?'

'Follow the rails and yer can't go wrong.'

Glen rose. 'Thanks. I figger I'll be a bit of a tenderfoot till I learn my way around.'

'I shore have a bad memory for names. What did you say yours was?'

'Glenister. Most folk calls me Glen.'

'Glen it shall be. Most folk calls me Smoke-stack on account of the hat I was wearing when I arrived here, but my mother christened me Franklyn. Don't yer worry about the job none. Yer'll soon get used to it. So long for now.'

'So long.'

Glen thoroughly enjoyed his meal with the Donovans. It was the first time he'd had his feet under a table in anyone's house for years. Donovan was delighted to know he was coming to work for the company.

'It's a good outfit to work for. They treat yer right. I ain't saying some of the muck slingers and the spike bashers ain't a bit ornery, but it's no more than yer kin expect. Most of 'em are straight out of Ireland and they've been fed on stories as how they only gotta get out west with a pick and shovel and a pan and they could dig all the gold they wanted. Some on 'em thought they'd find nuggets same as digging praties back home. When they get out here in the wilds and find the conditions they gotta work under, no wonder they get sore.'

He lit an old pipe and took two or three long pulls. 'Last winter we were on the plains and it wore shore bad. But up there in the mountains it's going to be plumb hell. I thank the Almighty that I'll be busy letting old Biddy roll. Biddy's tha name of my old coal burner, but I'm figgering it'll be wood we'll be feeding her on afore this winter's over.'

Glenister stayed yarning for another couple of hours. Before he took his leave of these kindly homely folk he promised to bring a baby cottontail for their small girl Kathleen, on his next visit to town — something she could have 'for her very own'.

The next morning, shortly after sun-up, he set out for the railhead camp, riding Rocky and leading a heavily laden pack mare. As he rode through the lonely country he thought over the chain of circumstances which had brought him to the present situation. Five hundred dollars a month was a hell of a lot of money for any cowhand to earn. A top rider was lucky if he got forty and 'found'. And it was the girl who'd been instrumental in getting him the job.

He drew rein on a spur of the mountains and took his first look at the scene of toil below him. As far as eye could see hundreds of men were working — mule teams hauling enormous wagons of timber ranging from railroad ties to wood needed for the shack town which was being built in the lee of the mountains.

The countryside echoed and re-echoed with the sound of blasting. Men, some stripped to the waist, swung fourteen-pound sledgehammers as they drove in the spikes which held the ties. Ahead of these, others shovelled rock and debris into wagons, and further on still, more workers hewed at the rock. Behind them stretched two gleaming steel rails — a railroad in the making.

A construction train of loaded cars was being pulled along these newly laid lines by a puffing and panting engine. Occasionally the engineer would blow his whistle to warn some solitary worker. From his position on the elevated ground, Glen could see some of the land which lay ahead. Huge canyons and gulches split the rising ground till the view was lost in the mist-covered topmost peaks of the High

Sierras, and beyond that lay the Feather River Valley. The way for more than a hundred and fifty miles into the wide plains of California.

In its upper reaches the Feather River is broad and green. Lower down, the water runs through a canyon cut deep through the red and brown rocks where the foam rises from the boiling rapids which man had never conquered.

It was through that canyon that Broomfield proposed to build his railroad. It was sure some chore, but it was not Glen's worry.

Lyttleton was waiting for him and took him, immediately on his arrival, to meet Grainger. Broomfield had obviously sent on his instructions, for after a few preliminary details, Glen was given a free hand.

'All I'm interested in, Glenister, is a steady flow of beef for my workers. Men can't work on empty bellies,' was his final remark, and Lyttleton took him to the butchers. It had been the custom for the meat contractors to deliver cows to the butchers through an agent, and for this reason they had to put up with whatever the agent liked to send.

Judging from the lean, scruffy stock which Glen saw in the makeshift corral, it was little wonder that the men had been discontented. Between them, the agent and the cattlemen had been on a good thing. The number normally slaughtered each week was about a hundred. Most of the workers fed in a communal chuck-house — married men with families were allowed a ration to take home.

More than five thousand head a year was a lot of cows. At the current price of twenty dollars a head, a heap of coin was involved. As Glen saw the situation, there was only one way to deal with the matter. That was for him to go out and about himself and to buy cows.

There was good range up here and with half a dozen reliable cowhands, the animals could be turned out until they were wanted. Once the winter was on them, things might be different and other arrangements would have to be made, but for the present his plan presented no difficulties. He put the suggestion to Lyttleton who, in turn, reported to Grainger and Glen received immediate approval and instructions to go ahead.

From then on he had little time to spare. Day after day he and Rocky were on the go. From Nevada to California he sought out ranchers and bought prime three-year-old steers. He collected an odd cowboy here and there till he had a nice outfit. All were men he could trust.

To trail cows up into the mountains would take too long, and it was decided that the hands should drive the stock to the nearest point which the track touched and they should then be loaded into freight cars and brought up to the camp. This was a great saving of time and much appreciated by Grainger.

Complaints from the workers became a thing of the past. Things ran smoothly until the first snows fell, then tempers were apt to get frayed. Little things that would normally pass unnoticed assumed gigantic proportions. A dry river-bed turned into a raging torrent overnight. The ground became a sea of mud where cursing mule skinners belaboured bogged-down teams.

Men, soaked to the skin and chilled to the marrow, cursed mule skinners for their inability to get the debris out of the way. Tracklayers were held up in consequence — the place was absolute chaos. Trains still got through and unloaded their freight, but the empty wagons accumulated — the ground was a morass.

Mule team after mule team went lame. The snow was not far off. Men demanded more free time so that they could go to town. When they got to Keedie they failed to return on the construction trains. Fights were an hourly occurrence and there was more than one killing. It was little wonder that everybody, from Theodore Broomfield downwards, became worried by the slow progress and the mounting costs.

Glen climbed down from a freight train and made his way along the cars to the one in which Rocky had travelled. The stallion had become an experienced railroad traveller, for Glen would go by freight train as far as possible on his visits to the distant ranches, returning by the same means when his business was concluded.

He was trying to build up a large herd and ranchers were loath to trail drive in the bad weather — many were miles away from the actual track.

Grainger, who was normally a placid man, came rushing up. 'Ah, Glenister, glad to see you're back. You're just the man I want. Know anything about mules?'

'Nary a thing, boss. Why?'

''Cos I just fired the boss mule skinner. I gotta have mules — plenty of 'em. Work's being held up right along the line because of the shortage of freight wagons. The wagons are here

— empty — and we can't get 'em loaded to send back, because the skinner reports there are more than fifty teams unfit for work. He ought to have seen this might happen and had a reserve. I want you to get away and buy mules.'

Glenister stared at him. He knew nothing of mules — his job was to buy beef.

'Me, boss? I know naught about the stubborn critters.'

'You know a horse better than anyone else in these parts, so you must know about mules. Anyways, Broomfield says for you to go south and buy mules. Good ones this time — animals that can stand up to the rigours we've got in front of us.'

Glen pushed back his hat and scratched his head. 'How many wore yer figgering on?'

'Two to three hundred. Come up to the office and I'll give you an order on the Bank to cover the cost.'

Without waiting to hear any more

from Glenister, he had gone. Three hundred mules! Where in tarnation was he going to find that number? Mules were not indigenous to these parts. The best he'd ever seen came from Missouri — that was a mighty long way off. These engineer fellows might know a heap about railroad building, but they hadn't got any notion on stock. They just said they wanted it and then expected it to be there.

After seeing Rocky fed and having a spot of chuck himself, he went in search of Lyttleton.

'Where'd they get the last mules from?' he asked.

'Half the teams were privately owned. The rest were bought in Missouri.'

Missouri. He'd thought as much. He'd have to go east via Salt Lake City and that meant going into Utah. There was still the Gorman business. He'd give two months' pay right now to know if he'd been accused of that killing.

A chance remark of a new engineer

gave him another idea. He'd overheard the man say that work had just about finished on a big dam north of Virginia City in Nevada. There would sure to have been mule teams on such a project.

Early next morning found him and Rocky on a freight train bound for that place. He found his mules, two hundred and eighty of the long-eared creatures, and thirty mule skinners.

But it was a long trail back and those mules were the most stubborn critters he'd ever had to contend with in the whole of his life. One day they'd make good time. Another and some of them would lie down without any justification and no amount of beating would get them on the move again till they felt like it.

At Virginia City days were lost by the non-arrival of the stock cars. When the cars eventually came, half the skinners were missing. It took Glenister and his outfit another day to round them up from the gold town's saloons.

When he arrived back at the railhead he found work had been completely stopped by the weather conditions. Grainger, however, was delighted to have the new teams and the additional drivers, though as the temperature was steadily falling, there was nothing to do but corral the mules and let the men push off down to Keedie.

8

It wanted six days to Christmas when Glen stamped the snow off his boots and pushed open the door of the Line End Saloon.

'Hyer, Glen, what'll it be?' asked Annie. ''Tain't often we sees yer in these parts.'

'Bourbon — and plenty of it.'

Annie had been passing the time of day with a dark man who was a stranger to Glen. She left him and came over to help Glen herself.

Glen glanced round the room. The cold had driven the customers around the roaring stove at the far end.

'No, I reckon not, marm,' Glen replied to her remark; 'and I wouldn't be here today except the big boss had been bawling me out. When it comes to ordinary things like buying beef, these 'ere railroad builders are the craziest galoots I ever dun met up with. They can't work themselves for the weather and yet they expect cowhands to drive stock when half the time they can't even see the critters — let alone find 'em. If they hadn't a-sent me high-tailing it over the whole blame State of Nevada for a bunch o' mules, I reckon the camp wouldn't be short o' beef right now.'

He downed his drink and helped himself to another.

'Yeah,' said Annie; 'I heard some of 'em bellyaching about it the other night.'

'It's all right them bellyaching when they sit around a stove! I'd like them to have a bit of what I've been through lately — hunting their doggorn beef.'

'Are yer looking fer beef, fella?' The question came from the stranger to whom Annie had been speaking when Glen came in.

'Looking! I'm snow-blind looking for the blame critters.'

'I think mebbe I could find yer five hundred head.'

Glenister McCreedie was in no mood for joking. 'Whose leg are yer trying to pull, mister?' he snarled. He was not amused. There weren't five hundred head to be had in a hundred-mile ride — at least not beef cows.

The man's face darkened. 'I ain't pulling yer leg, fella. I'm offerin' yer five hundred cows fer cash.'

Glen stared at him. He didn't like the looks of the fellow. He was a dark, swarthy, flashy type. His hands were not those of a hard-working cowman. But if, by chance, he did have some dogies for sale, five hundred would keep 'em going for nigh on a month.

'How much be yer asking fer these 'ere cows o' yourn, stranger, and where can they be seed?'

'Fifteen thousand dollars is the price, fella — in cash. And the cows will be waiting fer yer at Twin Forks when yer say.'

Twin Forks, thought Glen. He knew every cowman around there, but he didn't know of one with any stock to sell.

'Who's yer outfit?' he asked.

'We're a bunch o' strangers heading fer California and the winter's caught up on us. 'Tain't no use us trying afore spring.'

'These cows o' yourn must be prime stock if yer figgerin' on getting thirty bucks a piece for 'em.'

'That's the price, mister. Take it or leave it. I thought yer said this railroad was short o' beef.'

Glen laughed. Short of beef — he should say. 'So they are. But I ain't figgering on 'em eating gold just yet. Besides, what's this cash business? When ain't a draft on the W.P. been no good?'

'Fifteen thousand cash is the price.'

'Naught doing, mister. Ten thousand's my price — after inspection.'

The man studied Glen's face for a moment. 'It's a dicker. But yer gotta have the coin with yer. When yer want 'em at Twin Forks?'

'Three days' time will suit me.'

The man finished up his drink,

banged his glass on the bar, nodded to Glen and left the saloon.

'And who might that be, Annie?' Glen asked as the door swung-to behind him.

Annie shrugged her shoulders. 'Never seed him afore he blew in here two days back. That reminds me — there's another thing I had to tell yer. Two fellas and a good-looking dame were in here a week back. One of 'em was so mortally like you that I thought it was you, for a minute. The gal was a real high-stepper. They asked Charlie, the swamper, if he knew a Glenister McCreedie in these parts. He said he didn't. Shortly after they left and I seed 'em pull out. That gal rode her bronc same as any man. I told yer once afore, that if there's anything I can do — yer only gotta ask.'

She filled up Glen's glass and got one for herself.

'Thanks,' said Glen. 'One day I'll tell you a story, but I figger it'll keep for now. I gotta be heading back, the construction loco pulls out in ten minutes.'

He bid her so-long and made his way to the railroad depot. The snow was still falling and there was a bitter wind. He was glad to reach the shelter of the freight car.

Squatting on a sack of corn, he thought over all he'd heard. So, his family were catching up on him. The sooner they had a show-down, the better. When he'd been in Virginia City he'd read how the Harper gang had raided the jail where the kid had been held pending his trial and how he'd made his getaway.

Annie was a good old stick — she must know he was connected with that outfit in some way. If it became known who he was, he reckoned it would be the end of his job with the railroad. It would be a pity, for he liked the work and for once in his life he'd got money in the bank.

A couple of years and he'd have enough to buy a small spread. Still, it was no use worrying about it right now — he had to see about them cows.

That was another thing he didn't like. It smelt phoney to him, but he couldn't afford to miss anything in the way of beef, with the present state of affairs in the camp. Mebbe Grainger wouldn't have that amount of coin. If he did, Glenister would play safe and take the outfit with him in case of trouble.

The prospect of getting beef was too good to miss. Grainger was only too ready to let him have the coin. A freight train, with Jim Donovan as engineer, and a train crew were put at his disposal, and with the outfit as escort Glen set off.

He told Donovan of his misgivings and the train crew saw that their guns were loaded. Three miles out from Twin Forks they spotted the herd. This in itself was suspicious. An outfit with nothing to hide would have made straight for the junction where the loop rail could have been used for loading.

After the outfit had unloaded their horses, Glen handed the coin in its buckskin bag to Jim for safe keeping and told him to take the freight train on to the loop. If everything was O.K. he'd send back for the cash.

He checked his gun — he had never worn two in public since he had come into these parts. There had been no snow since the previous night — the going was firm and crisp and the horses got along without difficulty.

The man whom he had met in the Line End Saloon rode out to meet them. A second man, stoutish and black bearded, was with him. 'Howdy. Yer got the ten thousand with yer as we arranged?'

'Yeah. But I want ter see yer cows afore I parts with any coin.'

He rode over with them to the herd. The cows were there all right. Five hundred or possibly more, and with them eight or nine of the toughest hombres Glen had ever seen.

He rode on to make a closer

inspection. Many looked as if they were in calf, but what was more important to Glen, he saw three brands and he recognized them as those of nearby cowmen. This was rustled stock.

'Well, mister, do they suit?' the bearded man asked him.

Glen looked straight at him. 'I reckon not. The W.P. don't buy other folks' cows.'

The man flushed with anger. His voice was as icy as the wind that blew across the snow. 'Are yer claiming to call me a rustler, fella?'

'I ain't calling yer anything, mister. I'm just tellin' yer that I ain't a-buying stolen stock.'

The man's hand flew to his gun.

'Why you . . .'

But Glen was ready. With a deadly smoothness of movement his own iron was in his hand and it barked first.

Though the sound of the two shots had been almost simultaneous, Glen's was just a fraction of a second in advance and his bullet found its mark.

The shot aimed at him merely ploughed up the snow at Rocky's feet.

The sudden surprise scared the stallion — he spun round and the swerve saved Glen's life, for the other rustlers had gone for their guns. He felt a burning pain in his shoulder, and knew that he had been hit.

His gun again belched flame and a rustler toppled from his mount. Men fell on both sides.

Glen's wounded shoulder made him fumble as he tried to jam fresh shells into his gun.

'I shouldn't if I were you, fella.'

He knew that voice — sitting his mount less than a couple of feet away and with drawn gun, was his brother Roy. He had come up on Glen's blind side and the snow had deadened his approach.

Three of Glenister's riders were down — the remainder had their hands up. There was nothing else they could do. They were outnumbered by three to one.

Glen moved his eyes from his fallen riders and looked at Roy's handsome, smirking face.

'So it was the Harper gang,' he said quietly.

Roy laughed. 'Shore was, Glen. But I'm figgerin' it won't bear that name no longer. That galoot yer just downed was Harper. Yer long vacation ain't slowed yer up none. Purtiest draw I ever seed yer make. But don't get any fancy notion — all I want's the coin. Hand it over pronto and yer kin have the cows what yer came for.'

Glen could feel the blood running down his arm. The eyes of the other riders were on him.

'I ain't got no coin. It's on the train and there's mor'n half a dozen rifles guarding it. I figgered this might happen. You fellas must shore have thought us loco, if yer thought we'd bring that amount o' coin out to an outfit we'd never seen a-fore.'

As he spoke he saw the killer look in his brother's face.

'You liar,' Roy shouted; 'turn it over afore I forget who you are.'

Glen shrugged his shoulders and winced with pain. 'Search me, if yer don't believe me.'

From the distance they heard the whistle of the train. 'Don't be a crazy loon,' Glen whispered in an undertone that only Roy could hear. 'They heard the shooting. Get away — a-fore it's too late.'

Roy turned to the rustlers. 'I reckon this buzzard's got us licked. He ain't lying. I knowed him a-fore.'

'Put a slug into him,' cursed one of the gang.

Roy McCreedie turned on him like a tiger.

'Ain't there been enough killin' fer one day — d'yer want the whole country on our trail? This fella represents the railroad. I guess we'd better hightail it.'

'Shore had,' one of them agreed. 'That train's coming back.'

'What! And leave these cows behind,'

yelled an angry voice.

'Nary a thing else we kin do — split the breeze.' He turned again to Glen. 'You and me'll meet again, fella, and I'm figgerin' yer won't be so lucky next time.'

'Get out of the country,' Glen almost shouted at him; 'I saved yer neck once — but not again.'

Roy laughed and clapped spurs to his mount.

Leaving those that lay dead in the snow, the rustlers raced for the hills.

Jim Donovan and the train crew appeared, rifles in hand. They carried away the six dead men — three of Glen's outfit and three rustlers — and put the bodies aboard the train.

The wound in Glen's shoulder was roughly dressed. He decided to take the cows and settle with their rightful owners at a later date and they were loaded into the freight cars.

After making arrangements for the burying of the dead, Glenister reported to Theodore Broomfield himself. The first thing which the chief did was to insist that Glen's shoulder should be properly dressed. A sawbones was called — the wound probed and bound and he received strict instructions to lay up for a few days. Mrs. Donovan insisted that the time should be spent with her, and to the Donovans' shack Glen went.

The news of Harper's killing spread through the town like wildfire — once more Glenister was a public hero. The story of the fight was sent out over the railroad telegraph, and such details as the operator did not know he supplied from his imagination.

The tale grew by repetition and Glen awoke in the morning to find Jim Donovan guarding the door against two local reporters — one from the *Sentinel* and the other from its rival, the *Tribune*.

This was bad. The very last thing that Glenister McCreedie wanted was to have his name in print. Harper had committed crimes in three states

— California, Nevada and Utah. His death was news — big news. To the local one-man-owned news sheets it was the scoop of a lifetime. A personal interview with Harper's killer would fetch money with the large combines in Carson and Salt Lake City. Jim Donovan did his best, but the reporters were not to be gainsaid. As briefly as possible Glenister gave them the story.

On Christmas morning he refused to remain any longer in bed — he was no invalid. His little friend Kathleen was busily showing the presents which Santa Claus had brought her when another visitor was announced. No less a person than Miss Elizabeth Broomfield.

Glen had not met the lady since he had learned that he owed his present job to her. He felt somewhat embarrassed.

She smiled as she entered the room and held out her hand. 'Father is anxious to know how you feel this morning.'

'I'm mighty appreciative of the honour, marm. The doc tells me I was lucky. The bullet missed the bone, so I'm figgering on being back at camp come sun-up tomorrow. These good folk insist on me spending Christmas Day with them, or I'd have gone today.'

'That's quite right of Mrs. Donovan. Another day's holiday will do you good and I hope you'll enjoy some of the turkey you so thoughtfully sent in. Were the birds shot in the woods near here? I've never seen wild gobblers.'

Somehow she'd got to make this strange man talk. He fascinated her. His aloofness and his calm indifference to things on which other men set great store. His love for his horse.

Seeing him sitting here with the small child on his knee, it was hard to picture him as the man who'd killed the most notorious outlaw in the State. She was convinced that he was a man without fear and yet capable of great love and understanding.

But over and above all this he gave

her the impression of a man who was never off his guard — as if he were always listening and looking for something behind him.

Even now his gunbelt was hung on the back of his chair. Yet she could not remember that he had worn one at their first meeting.

'There's nothing like the sight of a bunch of gobblers on the run,' he told her. 'Anything from thirty to a hundred of 'em, with their red necks stuck out and their bronze bodies scurrying along. Some of the old 'uns weigh thirty to forty pounds. I aimed to see the outfit had a Christmas dinner, so me and my boys went up into the woods hunting and I reckon we were lucky. In one day we got close on to three or four hundred birds. My folks used to figger on it weren't Christmas without turkey. But I guess, living with 'em all around, it weren't no treat to us kids.' He sighed as he thought of his long days without freedom.

'You love the wild and the wild things

160

in it, don't you?' she asked.

'Shore do, marm. I wore raised in sight of the Sierras and I get lonesome without 'em around.'

Elizabeth Broomfield shuddered. Glenister McCreedie looked at her closely — she didn't look like a shallow sort of girl who'd only be interested in towns and the bright lights and so on. Why didn't she like the Sierra country?

'You don't like 'em?' he asked.

'I hate this country. I hate its ruthlessness and its savagery. I hate the lawlessness of its people. But I love its beauty and the hospitality of some of its people. There is something about it that grips you and holds you, although at the same time you fear it.'

Glen had never heard anyone talk like this. He liked her voice — he wanted her to go on.

'I guess, marm, yer worn't raised here. Shore it's wild. And I guess to an Easterner, us folks are like savages. Only a few years back it wore only the Indians that lived here. It's the mountains and the forests that have made us what we are. If yer want anything up here — yer've gotta go out and get it. It's what the fellas that writes books calls the law of the jungle — the survival of the fittest. Up here, when a human or an animal critter's hungry, he goes out and he kills to eat. He don't kill mor'n he wants. An animal with a full belly will drink at the same stream as the fella he was hunting when he was hungry. It's the human critter with his greed and lust for wealth that does the harm. Out on the plains it wore the buffalo hunter. He slaughtered the beasts in hundreds just for the price of their hides. In the forests it wore the trappers that wanted the furs for the purty ladies back East.'

He stopped his harangue suddenly. He had been on a pet subject and he had let his feelings run away with him. 'I apologize, marm. I was letting this old tongue of mine run away with me.'

Jim Donovan had come into the room — he had listened intently to all

Glenister had had to say. He was a queer fellow, this guest of theirs. He talked like a book, but to look at him you'd have thought he was just a hard-bitten Westerner.

Jim was an Irishman himself and he had all the poetry and love of nature and beautiful things that is the curse (or the blessing?) of the Celt. He had not expected to find the same traits in the folk out West.

'Please go on,' said Elizabeth Broomfield, 'I'm interested in your point of view.'

Glenister McCreedie pulled out his sack of Durham and rolled himself a cigarette. The embarrassment which he had at first felt when Elizabeth had come into the room, was forgotten. The emotions he had experienced during his three years in the penitentiary, when the deprivation of his freedom had been a far greater punishment to bear than any laborious task, found expression in a passionate defence of the wild country and its native population.

He hadn't liked Elizabeth Broomfield — he had resented her friendly approach at the time of the train hold-up. She represented the East and the people who were bringing the ways of the East to the unspoiled, unconquered West. Yet, in some indefinable way he found comfort in talking to her.

'Then the pioneers came, the settlers and the gold seekers. They all wanted something. And now it's the railroads.'

Jim Donovan stared at him. The railroads? Surely he wasn't against the railroads. The railroads were providing work for thousands of folk.

'But you ain't against the railroads, are you?' he asked.

'No, I ain't. I'm only trying to explain to Miss Broomfield the ways of the West. Up here, might is right and the weak go to the wall. Or these days, they're crushed in the scramble for wealth.'

'If you think my father is one of those who only want wealth from the West, you are wrong,' Elizabeth took up the challenge. 'He is a builder — a creator of something in which he believes. In spite of ill-health he is determined to carry on, even if it costs him his life. I have seen his health deteriorating every day as he pits himself against the seemingly impossible. Do you wonder I hate the country? There is no necessity for me to remain here — I could go back East tomorrow. But as long as my father stays, I stay. You may be right about man's greed for wealth. But remember that in the East there are thousands of people who have barely enough to live on. Out here there are miles and miles of land which could be put to good use. Without such men as my father it would remain the home of the wild things that you love — it would be of no use to any but those who already live here. The railroad will give you the chance to send your products to the Eastern markets. What I hate about it is the uncivilized way in which you live — the way in which you settle your arguments with bullets.'

Glen felt the blood rise to the roots of his hair. So this was the truth of the matter. She looked on him as a gunman — mebbe a killer. He didn't feel like defending himself. She wouldn't understand. All the same he wasn't prepared to take it sitting down.

'That's where yer wrong, marm, if I may say so. Yer've gotta fight for anything yer want — same as yer paw's gotta fight Feather River if this railroad's to go through. Same as the settler and the cowman's gotta fight the weather, snow or drought and the rustlers. A fella's gotta fight even for peace of mind. And if yer ain't up to it — well, then yer've gotta get out or go under.'

Elizabeth Broomfield's firm mouth set in a straight line. A gleam of anger came into her blue eyes.

'Perhaps I don't see it in the same way as you do. When I've been here longer, perhaps I might change my opinion. But I hate killing, even when it's a necessity. Thank you for a very interesting conversation. I must get back to my father. He will be wondering what has become of me. Good-bye. He will be glad to hear that you have recovered.'

Glen got up from his chair. 'Thank you, marm. I've shore enjoyed our pow-wow. If ever you think of taking a look at them old gobblers, I'll be shore proud to show you.'

Jim Donovan saw her to the door of the shack. 'A fine young lady,' he said when he came back to Glen.

'She shore is. But I reckon she don't approve of my ways. It ain't likely an Easterner would. I'm figgerin' it's going to be hard on her up here.'

9

Glen's shoulder healed slowly. The weather became worse. A raging northeast blizzard brought blinding snow. The temperature fell to fifteen degrees below zero.

The inhabitants of Keedie, huddled round their stoves, yarned and grumbled — cursed and fought. Huge drifts blocked the passes and work came to a standstill.

The trains to the south still ran, but they were sometimes days late and had to be dug out. Food was getting short all round, both in the town and in camp. Some of the married workers, who had built shacks for themselves and their families, were cut off and nearly starving.

More and more work fell on Glen's shoulders. He arranged rescue parties and many families blessed his name.

Glenister had begun to respect these railroad pioneers. Back in camp he saw them daily as they pored over drawings and wrestled with mathematical problems of elevations, strains and stresses.

He marvelled at their skill, but sometimes doubted the accuracy of their deductions when he came across a trestle bridge which had been swept away, or collapsed under the enormous weight of fallen snow. Fighting Mother Nature was sure some chore. But when things went wrong, these men did not give in. They just got down to it and tried something else.

Lyttleton gave him a further insight into the picture which probably explained the anxiety that showed on Broomfield's face. The Chief grew more haggard every day. It appeared that the bankers in San Francisco were jibbing at sinking more capital — the debenture and other stockholders were impatient to see some results for their investment. Their backers, the Denver and Rio Grande Railroad, had not the huge resources of the Southern

Pacific. It was not only the difficulties of the terrain that Broomfield had to overcome.

Glen began to understand why Elizabeth Broomfield hated it all so. She knew that worry was killing her father.

The blizzard died down, the snow froze hard. His shoulder had almost healed and transport and food problems were settled for the time being.

He chafed at having so little to occupy his time in the camp.

He bought a pair of snow-shoes and some traps and spent days in the woods. His bag made a welcome change to the monotonous menu of beef.

On one of his hunting trips he had spotted several silver foxes. They were rare in this part of the country. He determined to trap them and give the skins to the Broomfield girl. Day after day he found a common grey fox or a coyote in his traps. One morning as he went his rounds he found that his luck had changed — a beautiful dog fox with a silver coat lay dead in the trap. A week later he caught another. With meticulous care he stretched and dried the pelts so that the silver-streaked fur retained its perfection.

Even while he worked he wondered at himself. What was this girl to him? An Easterner — a girl who hated the country, the daughter of a wealthy railroad man. He shrugged his shoulders. Oh well, he owed her something for getting him the job. She'd probably throw them back at him — she hated 'killing'.

A few days later, with the furs under his arm, he boarded a loco and headed for town. He made his way directly over to the Chief's special car. Miss Broomfield was out. He left the parcel and padded off through the snow to the Donovans' shack. He had brought three grey fox skins for Maw Donovan and little Kathleen. He knocked — the door was opened by Elizabeth Broomfield.

'Howdy, marm. I just left a parcel fer yer at yer car.'

She stared at him coldly. Her manner was frigid. What had he done this time?

'For me?' There was no friendliness in the tone of the question. She stepped aside to make way for him to enter.

Maw Donovan sat by the stove with baby Kathleen on her knee. She looked as if she had been crying.

Glen stared from one to the other of the women. 'What's wrong?' he asked.

Maw Donovan answered him: 'It's Jim. He got into a fight last night. The doc thinks he's hurt bad. It's his head.'

Glen was amazed. 'Jim? In a fight? He ain't the fightin' sort. What was the fracas about?'

'He won't say. But perhaps he might tell you. Go in and see him, but don't wake him if he's asleep.'

'Thank you, marm, I will. It don't seem the right time for gifts, but I brought these furs for you and young Kath — they'll keep yer warm, I reckon.' He pushed a parcel into her hands and went into the other room.

Jim was not asleep. He lay very still and his head was bandaged.

'Howdy, fella. Who'd yer tangle with?'

Jim's face was like a piece of raw beef. His eyes were black and blue. A bandaged arm rested on the blankets.

'That you, Glen? I'm glad yer got in. It wore that boss mule skinner that Grainger fired. He wore blowing his big mouth off about you and what he wore going to do ter yer, the first time he met up with yer without guns. It stuck in my craw and I ups and give him a piece of my mind.'

Donovan drew a deep breath and tried to shift into a more comfortable position. 'We come to blows. And, Glen, he's a dirty fighter. He got me in the groin with his boot. I reckon I must have hit my head — 'cos I don't remember no more till I wore back here. It's the wife and the youngster I'm worrying about. They'll have naught comin' in if I'm off work long.'

As Glenister listened to the story he had been thinking — was this the reason that Elizabeth Broomfield had seemed so unfriendly? But why should she connect him with the fight? Mrs. Donovan had said that Jim refused to tell them anything about it. Still, right now he must put Jim's mind at rest.

'Nary you worry about that, old timer. I got enough coin fer the four of us. And we'll have yer pushing old Biddy along again in no time. Where d'yer run across this fella?'

'In the Silver Spike. He and a bunch of his pards hang out there. Listen, Glen — don't shoot the critter on my account and fer heaven's sake don't tangle with yer fists. That shoulder o' yourn can't be right yet.'

Glen laughed, though his face was stern — his lips straight. 'O.K., Jim. Just leave it ter me. I'll be back.'

He went into the room where he had left Elizabeth and Mrs. Donovan.

'Pardon me, ladies. I gotta see a fella. I'll be right back.'

As he made for the door, Elizabeth barred his way. 'John Glenister, where are you going?'

'I dun told yer, marm. I gotta see a fella.'

'I suppose you're going to look for the man who beat Jim up. Fighting, fighting — can you never think of anything else?'

'Shore, marm. But right now yer gotta excuse me.'

'John Glenister, if you kill that man I will never speak to you again.' Her lips were a thin straight line — her eyes blazed with baffled rage.

'I reckon yer know yer own mind best, marm.' With that Glen turned on his heel and walked out of the cabin.

The Silver Spike Saloon was one that he seldom frequented. It was used mostly by C.P. hands when they hit town. The place was crowded when he pushed open the doors. He stood slowly pulling off his gloves as he looked round the room. A hush fell over the company as they became aware of his presence.

He saw the mule skinner, in the company of three other men, sitting at a table by the wall. As Glen approached the man looked up. An expression of fear came into his eyes. 'I ain't gotta gun,' he screamed. He kicked the chair away and backed to the wall.

Glen advanced in silence till he was less than a foot away. The gloves that he held in his left hand struck the man across the face.

'You yellow skunk. Yer used ter tote a gun when yer wore at the camp — get it.'

'I won't. It'd be murder. What chance would I have against you? I ain't no gun-slick.'

The only sound in the room was that of men breathing. You could have heard a pin drop. Glen's hand hung over his gun. He was in a cold fury. He was afraid his temper would get out of control.

He called to three fellows whom he knew as bosses on the track: 'Hey you, Murphey, Carey, Watson. Watch my back. We'll see if this skunk can do to one of his own age and size what he's done to an old man.'

A mean wicked look replaced the fear in the man's eyes. Glen slipped out of his sheepskin storm-breaker and unbuckled his gunbelt. He handed the things to Murphey.

In height and build there was little to choose between the two men. Both were big, tough and without an ounce of superfluous fat. Tables and chairs were pushed out of the way. The company formed a ring.

Glen had barely stepped forward when the skinner rushed straight at him swinging both arms as if he were urging on his mules. A straight left brought him to an abrupt halt. Glen's right cracked on his jaw. It was a hard blow — one that would have dropped many a man, but not this one.

He shook his head and came on. Another left hit him above the eyes — it did not stop him and a tremendous left cracked Glen across the side of the head. It made him realize the strength of this gorilla.

He reeled back, his ears ringing. The skinner's supporters yelled encouragement. He came in again, but a well-timed right to the midriff made him grunt. Another right smashed him in the mouth and brought first blood.

Glen's training in Rocky Point was standing him in good stead. His old instructor had always said, 'Follow yer man up once yer got him going. Never give him time to recover.' And Glen did just this. He belted his man across the head twice with his left and sank another into his breadbasket.

But this mule skinner was tough — mighty tough. Back he came and this time it was Glen who stopped a lovely right to the mouth. It jolted his head back and brought him on to his heels. For a second he was fuzzy, but the feeling passed and he waded back into the skinner. The man had no skill — he was relying on sheer brute force to get him by.

Glen caught a beautiful right bang on his nose. The blood literally squirted out. Both men were bleeding from mouth and nose. Another left from Glen got the skinner in the eyes and a right sent his head back. So far there could be no mistake as to which man was taking the licking.

The onlookers were yelling like a pack of fiends. The noise had brought others from outside. The saloon was packed to its doors and faces were pressed against the frosty windows in a desperate effort to see what was happening.

Time and time again Glen drove his opponent back, but the fellow was as tough as the mules he drove. Glen caught him with a right that had every ounce of his two hundred pounds behind it. The skinner spat out three teeth — he was groggy on his feet.

Here was Glen's chance. Throwing caution to the winds, he sailed in to finish him off. But the man had realized his danger. Going back till he was almost among the spectators, he flung a kick that caught Glen low in the groin.

Until then he had fought fair. But in frontier towns it was 'free for all' and Glen should have been on his guard. A nauseating pain went through his whole body — he went down in agony. A high-laced boot studded with steel nails was more than any man could stand.

A fiendish look of joy came over the skinner's features and through a mist of pain, Glen saw the boot go back for another kick. Somehow, though he never knew how, he squirmed out of the way. His two hands grabbed the out-stretched leg and with a tremendous heave that sent waves of pain through his wounded shoulder, he sent the skinner crashing among the watching crowd.

He had gained a momentary, sorely needed respite. He dragged his pain-wracked body up from the floor and stood swaying drunkenly from side to side. The skinner scrambled to his feet. With head down, he rushed forwards like an infuriated bull. They were no longer human beings — they were beasts mad with pain, with all reason gone.

As the man hurled himself forward in his mad charge, Glen side-stepped and caught him a terrific blow behind the ear. He went sprawling to the ground, but nothing would keep him down. He got to his feet, his breath coming in short gasps.

Regardless of the blows which Glen rained on him, he gripped his middle in a bear-like hug and both men fell with a thud that shook the floor.

Over and over they rolled, each straining every muscle to crush the life out of his adversary. Glen could feel the hot liquor-stinking breath of the skinner on his face as they clawed for one another's throats.

Panting, black with sweat, with shirts torn to ribbons, locked together they clambered to their feet — only to crash again to the floor, this time with the skinner uppermost.

Glen sensed that the man was trying

to jab his fingers into his eyes. He gripped the descending arm. Slowly the skinner's greater strength was beginning to tell. Savagely his fingers groped for Glen's eyes.

Exerting every bit of strength in his pain-wracked body, Glen drew up his knees and with one final effort forced the hulking body from him.

The spectators, appalled by such an exhibition of bestial cruelty, shuffled back out of the way. Slowly Glen forced back the man's arm — sweat was pouring down their faces. Back and further back it went. The veins stood out on the tortured man's brow. Glen saw fear in his eyes — stark fear. An overwhelming wave of black rage came over him. This man was at his mercy and, as he thought of Donovan he increased the pressure. There was a scream from the skinner. Glen felt the bone snap. The arm went limp.

With the breaking of his arm the skinner's resistance crumpled and collapsed like a house of cards. He slumped forward on to Glen in an inert heap. Heaving the body from him, Glen staggered to his feet. He looked down at the jibbering, broken thing which a second or two before had been a man.

He wiped the back of his hand across his blood-covered face in an attempt to clear away the figures which danced before his eyes. He stared at the awe-struck onlookers. Sanity was returning to his throbbing head. He staggered drunkenly and turned towards the bar.

A lane opened through the crowd and, swaying, he lurched across the room. He would have fallen had he not caught hold of the bar ledge.

'Give me a drink,' he croaked. His throat felt parched — his breath was coming in short gasps.

The terrified bartender slid over a bottle and glass.

Glen ignored the glass, picked up the bottle and drank deeply. The raw spirit revived him. With staring eyes and bottle in hand, he glared at the company.

'Next time that galoot wants a fight mebbe he'll think twice. Go get a sawbones, one of yer. He needs one.'

Murphey crossed the room to his side and held out the coat and gunbelt. Mechanically he buckled on the belt and got into his coat. Men, including the bartender, spoke to him. He did not answer. He took another drink from the bottle and staggered through the door into the cold air.

He was almost at the Donovans' door when he remembered the Broomfield girl's words — 'John Glenister, if you kill that man I will never speak to you again.' He stopped in his tracks. Folks on the sidewalk were staring at him. He turned and headed back. He staggered into the Line End Saloon. Somewhere inside him a voice was saying: 'She must never see you like this.'

The next thing he knew was that he found himself lying on something soft. His head throbbed and there was something wrong with his mouth. He opened his eyes and looked around him.

Where was he? In a room that he had never seen before. The furniture was ornate — gilt. He was on a couch and someone had thrown blankets over him.

He raised himself on his elbows and winced with pain. His whole body ached — he was not aware what part hurt the most. The room went round and round. Gradually things began to come back to his mind. He'd had a fight with the boss mule skinner.

He threw off the blankets. He realized that he'd hurt his wounded shoulder. A mirror was hanging on the wall on the opposite side of the room. He saw his reflection. What a mess! His eyes were black — great finger claw marks ran down the length of one cheek. His lips were swollen to twice their size. He got to his feet — he must have a closer look. But the floor rose and fell like the swell of the sea and he had to sit on the side of the couch. He felt as if he'd been trampled under the hoofs of a hundred cows.

The door of the room opened. Annie came in. She was carrying a jug of steaming coffee.

'So you've come round, have yer? Here, drink this — it will do yer good.'

So he was in Annie's saloon, was he?

'How'd I get here and what'm I doing in yer room?'

'Yer walked here on yer own two feet. But lord knows how yer dun it after what yer musta bin through. I'm figgering yer were out on yer feet when yer staggered into the bar. There wore a bunch o' scared galoots behind yer, but nary one had the guts to speak to yer or give yer a hand.'

Glen took the cup she held out to him. His hand shook like a cotton-seed dancing in the breeze.

'Lor', anyone seeing me would think I'd been on a drunk for a month.' The coffee was too hot, but it tasted good.

'What happened?' he asked.

'Yer mumbled something about 'she must not see me like this' and passed out. I had yer brought in here and I sent for Doc Manners. The critter ain't showed up yet. So I tried to clean yer up a bit, myself. Yer shore wore a sight.'

Glen gulped down some more of the hot coffee. 'That wore shore mighty good of yer, Annie, and I appreciates it.'

'Forget it, fella. But it musta been some fight. Harry's just come back from looking for the doc. He tells me he'll be right over as soon as he's finished with the fella yer tangled with.'

Again Elizabeth Broomfield's words rang in Glen's ears. 'Is he bad hurt — he ain't going ter die, is he? I reckon I saw red when that buzzard booted me.'

Annie shrugged. 'How'd I know? I ain't seed him. But the doc'll put yer mind at rest when he gets here. It ain't the other fella I'm thinking about — it's you. Yer shore keep this old town alive with yer doings. First it wore the train hold-up. Then yer top that hoss and then yer plugged Harper. And now it's this 'ere fight. The saloon's packed.

They know yer in here and like most of the two-faced critters they are, they're wanting to clap yer on the back.

'I ain't saying it ain't natural, for Jim Donovan was well liked and the way that fella beat him up wore something awful. It fair turned my innards when they told me and I ain't weak in them parts as I knows. But I reckon yer've settled accounts for all times. Them that wore there said when yer finished with him, he wore like a jibbering half-wit. He wore blubbering on the floor like a whipped hound dog.'

There was a tap on the door and the doc bustled in. For an instant he stared at Glen. Then he turned to Annie. 'Why, woman, from the message I got, I thought this fella was nigh on dying and I find him drinking coffee in a lady's sanctum!'

'Keep yer blather fer yer other tame cats, Manners. I knows whether a fella needs a sawbones or not.'

The doc grinned at her. 'My, my, what's got into yer?' He winked at

Glen. 'What about finding me a drop o' that special bourbon while I look at my patient?'

Railroad Annie snorted. She made no comment and flounced out of the room. Doc Manners smiled at Glen. 'So that's that. I tell yer, Glen, the older yer get, the less yer knows about the female critters. Yer can't please 'em no ways. Well, let me have a look at yer. Kin yer get outa yer shirt? It ain't the cuts and bruises I'm worrying about — it's the shoulder. I'm figgering fighting ain't the best treatment for it.'

Glen struggled out of his shirt — not without pain. 'How's the other fella?' His voice showed his anxiety.

'He's in bad shape, but he ain't going to die — not just yet awhile. But you shore made a nasty mess of him. I knowed yer wore strong, but how yer broke that forearm bone with yer hands, beats me.'

As he talked the doc was examining Glen's wounded shoulder. 'Dang it — as I feared yer've opened up that wound. What else has he done to yer?'

Glen told him about the kick in the groin.

'I wore expecting that. It's that gent's favourite form of attack. He dun it to Donovan.'

'How is Jim, doc?' Glen asked.

'It's hard to say. I reckon that in falling he cracked the base of his skull. But without hospital equipment I can't be sure. As far as his other injuries are concerned, he'll be well in a couple of weeks. But I can only tell about his head with time.'

He went on with his examination of Glen. Finally he gave a satisfied grunt.

'Yer badly bruised, fella. But I don't think there's any bad injury.'

Glen struggled back into his shirt. He was thinking of Donovan and the mule skinner.

'Send Jim's bills to me, doc. I'll pay for any treatment yer consider's necessary. If needs be, send him up to one of these hospitals. I'll let yer have the coin. And that goes fer the mule skinner too.'

The doc was busy putting his instruments away. He looked at Glen with a puzzled expression. 'Yer a queer mixture of a man, Glenister. Yer beat a man nigh to death and then yer worry about him. I'm telling yer that mule skinner'll never be the same again. I don't mean physically, but mentally. When yer licked him yer broke his spirit. I ain't saying he didn't deserve it — 'cos he did. It's the same as yer broke that wild hoss o' yourn.'

Glen laughed. 'That's where yer wrong, doc. Rocky's spirit ain't broken. Him and me understand one another — that's all. I respect him, but if it comes to a showdown he knows I'm his master. No, doc. It's other things that breaks a fella up. Things like being shut up and losing yer self-respect. Mebbe it's yer pride that's hurt.'

For a minute the doc studied him in silence. 'That's what's happened to yer in the past, isn't it, son?'

Glen picked up an empty coffee cup and twisted it round and round in his hand. He sighed and then looked directly at the doc's face. 'We weren't talking about me, doc.'

'I know. But what I'm trying to tell yer's this — in future men will point at that mule skinner and say, 'That's the fella Glenister licked.' It's his pride and his prestige that's gone. Folks are made different. Some can get over a licking — others can't. They let it prey on their minds. Either they go on being licked curs or they let it sour their souls and they become cowardly snakes. The type that will shoot a fella in the back, or stick a knife into him when he's asleep. Yer've made a bad enemy in that fella. One that will stick at nothing to get his own back.'

'I reckon I see what yer mean. Thanks. I appreciate the warning.'

The doc smiled. 'Now, I reckon,' he said, 'a couple of hours on that there fancy couch of Annie's won't do yer no harm.'

Annie returned with a bottle and three glasses on a tray. 'How bad's he hurt?' she asked.

'There's nothing wrong with him that rest won't put right. I've just been telling him that a couple of hours on that couch is what he needs right now.'

Annie set down the tray. 'That's all right by me. Get yerself down, Glen, and when yer wake I'll have the cook get yer some chuck.' She smiled at the doc. 'Here's the drink yer wanted, old guzzle-guts.' She poured out three glasses and handed them round.

'Now that's what I call hospitality.' The doc laughed as he downed his in one go. He smacked his lips. 'That's more like bourbon. The rot-gut you sell out there fair burns a man's innards.'

'I ain't noticed there's much wrong with yer innards and yer've had yer share,' Annie retorted.

After another glass the doc left and she turned to Glen. 'Get yer boots off and curl up,' she ordered. 'The doc's right. It's sleep yer want. And stop thinking about that Broomfield girl. Yer ain't killed the fella.'

Glen looked at her — what did she know?

'Who says I'm worrying about her?'

'I says so. A fella in the state you wore when yer come in here, don't babble about a woman if he ain't got her on his mind. I tell yer, Glen, though mebbe it ain't my business, she's not your sort. What does a gal that's lived East in a city all her life, know about us folk that live on the frontier? I ain't saying that she ain't pleasant enough, 'cos she talk'd to me — a scarlet woman that runs a saloon.'

'Who calls yer a scarlet woman?'

'Lots does — behind my back, but not to my face. I bin around, Glen — I know. Sometimes I wonders if I ain't crazy. I got all the coin I wants. I could buy a nice house in 'Frisco, but what would I do with myself? I can't figger me talking nice and fancy to a bunch o' dames.'

Glen looked at her carefully. Until that time he had always seen Railroad Annie with a smile on her face — a good-natured 'hail-fellow-well-met' sort of expression. Now she looked older and somewhat sad.

'Ain't yer ever married, Annie?' he asked.

'What chance has a dance-hall gal got?' She laughed, but there was a trace of bitterness in her tone. 'There was a fella once. He wore an engineer. He allus said he didn't care what I'd been and he meant it.' She had a faraway look in her eyes — one that few of her customers had ever seen.

'What happened to him — or shouldn't I ask?'

'He wore killed by a fall of rock when they wore building the Denver and Rio Grande. No, Glen, I ain't the marrying sort.' She got up and prepared to leave the room. 'But there, just listen to me rattling on about things that happened twenty years ago. You get yourself settled down.' She threw more logs on the stove and as she left the room Glen realized that he was not the only person who had a past.

10

Glen woke to find Annie shaking him. The ache in his head had gone.

'Glen, get up — Glen, do yer hear me?' He rolled over and sat up.

'Shore, shore. What's wrong?'

'Listen, Glen — there's Hank Taylor the sheriff and two strangers out there asking fer yer. They know yer here and they looks like badge toters to me.'

Glenister was wide awake by this time. So it had come — they'd caught up with him. But this was California. He reached for his gunbelt that had been hanging on the back of a chair and buckled it on. He checked the load and saw that the trigger rested on an empty cylinder.

Fear showed in Annie's eyes. 'What yer aiming ter do, son? Yer ain't figgerin' on shooting it out with three of 'em? Whatever it is they want yer for

— go without putting up a fight. I'll get yer sprung somehows.'

Glen was tying down his holster string. 'I dun three years in Rocky Point for a crime I didn't commit. I'm a convict on parole. The night you left Salt Lake City a man was shot in my arms. The fella was a prison guard that I'd never liked, but I didn't have no hand in his killing. They'll pin it on me all the same. I ain't going back. Thanks fer all yer've dun. It's been nice knowing yer. If they get me, look after Rocky.' He pulled a sheaf of bills from a money belt under his shirt. 'Give these to Doc. It's to pay for Donovan's hospital treatment.'

Annie shook her head. 'Put it away, son. I'll see to that. You might want it if yer on the run.'

He put his arm round her and kissed her on the cheek. Then he got into his coat and clamping his hat on the back of his head, he went into the saloon. Annie followed close at his heels.

The sheriff and the two strangers

were propping up the bar. Glen made straight for them.

'Howdy, sheriff. Annie tells me yer want ter see me.'

'Shore do.' He stopped and stared at Glen's battered face. 'Doggorn it, Glenister, from the looks of yer that musta bin a hell of a fight yer had.'

'Shore was. I feels as if I'd been trampled on by a five-hundred-pound steer.'

The two men who'd accompanied the sheriff smiled. The sheriff motioned towards them.

'This is a law officer from Carson City, Glenister, and this is another from Salt Lake. They come up here specially ter see yer.'

Glen's face became a stiff mask.

'Now don't be getting any fool notion in yer head,' the sheriff chuckled. 'It's shore pleasant business they've come about. Mighty pleasant fer yer. I'm figgering yer didn't know there were a heap o' coin on Harper's head. These gents are here ter give yer a couple o'

Bank Drafts fer nigh on ten thousand dollars. If yer'll step along ter my office, we kin get down ter signing the papers.'

For a fraction of time the eyes of Glenister McCreedie and Railroad Annie met. She was the first to recover her composure.

'Well, I reckon, Glen, that's mighty good news. It calls fer a drink. What'll it be, fellas?'

'Whiskey, marm, thankee.' Glen felt the sweat running under his collar. He had a funny feeling in the pit of his stomach and a tingling at the back of his knees. What with relief and surprise, he was at a loss for words. He swallowed hard and pulled himself together.

'Shore. What'll it be?'

Annie laughed. 'I reckon yer too late, fella. I figger yer good fortune's taken yer breath away.'

'How right yer are. But I don't rightly know that I cottons to the notion of taking reward money.'

'That's loco talk,' said the sheriff, glass in hand. 'Where'd yer be if that slug yer stopped had been a mite lower? No, sir. Yer shore rubbed out a bad critter if ever there was one. The only trouble is, his gang's still left. Only a coupla days ago news come through that they had stuck up a bank in Virginia City.'

'That's true enough,' the law man from Carson chimed in. 'They killed the cashier and got away with twenty thousand. There's some plumb funny stories going around about that gang. A rancher in Nevada claims they took possession of his place during a storm and he reckons the boss o' the outfit's a woman — young and good looking. He says she handles a bronc and a gun good as any man.'

He put down an empty glass and Annie filled it again. After a good gulp the man continued his tale. 'We asked him what he'd been drinking that night, for none of us never heard of Harper having any kin, let alone a gal. But this 'ere old cowman still says it wore a woman.'

Glen insisted on having another couple of rounds. Then he went with the three of them to sign and collect the Bank Drafts. When the necessary formalities had been completed he went back to the Line End Saloon.

He wanted to catch the last work train back to camp that night, but before doing so there were one or two chores that had to be done. He found Annie as much relieved as he had been himself. She was a good friend, this one-time dance-hall girl. He left the Bank Drafts with her and went off to see Doc Manners.

He wanted to make it certain that if Donovan needed city hospital treatment he should have it — all the doc had to do was to collect the money from Annie.

His next call was at the Donovan's shack. Maw Donovan was shocked at his appearance. Jim was easier and asleep. The news of the fight had reached them.

'It was funny, Glen. As soon as Jim

heard, he smiled and said: 'I figgered it would be like that. Thank heaven he didn't use a gun,' and then he went to sleep. Miss Broomfield was different. She took it bad. All she said was, 'Such brutes.' But I could see by her face how she felt. Yer see, Glen, she don't understand how us folks live.'

'I reckon mebbe yer right, marm. As I told her once afore she ought ter leave the West to folks that knows its ways. Squeamish Easterners ain't the sort that'll ever understand us. I reckon it ain't her fault. She ain't had ter fight ter live.'

The train whistled from the siding. Glen took a bunch of bills from his pocket.

'Get Jim anything he wants and if Doc Manners wants him ter go ter the city, you and Kath go with him. I fixed everything up. If anything goes wrong, send word ter me and I'll come a-running.'

'Gawd bless you, John Glenister.' Before she could say more the door had closed and he was gone.

The following morning Doc Manners set off on his round. He dropped in to see Broomfield, who had been his patient since making Keedie his head-quarters. He found him with Elizabeth finishing a late breakfast.

'Ah, Manners. Just the man I wanted to see. You can give me the lowdown on this fight Glenister was in with that mule skinner. I mean that fella that beat up Donovan. I've sent for the sheriff. I won't have my employees attacked in that way. The sheriff is paid to keep law and order and if he is incapable of fulfilling his duties, then someone else must be found.'

Doc Manners pulled out a chair — sat down and laughed. 'After the beating Glenister gave that mule skinner, I don't think he'll cause you any more trouble for some time to come.' He went on to describe all that he knew of the fight.

Broomfield was a fair man, a sportsman and furthermore he loved a good fight. As the doc told the story, his grim face relaxed into smiles. Miss Elizabeth, on the other hand, looked horrified and disgusted.

'Such beasts,' she exclaimed. 'They're lower than beasts. Beasts, at least, only fight to live.' She stopped suddenly. She remembered that it was Glenister himself that had made that remark.

'My dear,' said her father, 'here on the frontier, where men gamble daily with their lives, you've got to expect such things. It's men like Glenister who are the backbone of the West. They believe in right. If a man suffers an injustice they take the law into their own hands.

'If they waited for the law to take its course, nine times out of ten the miscreants would get off scot free. The evildoers believe that might is right. I'm sorry to have to admit it, but from my experience of the West, there's often a bunch of unscrupulous men dominating a whole town or countryside.'

Elizabeth Broomfield tightened her

lips and shook her head.

'It's no use, father, you won't change me. A man who goes out deliberately looking for a fight, as John Glenister did, is nothing but a beast and a savage to my way of thinking.'

Doc Manners took up the cudgels. He liked what he'd seen of John Glenister. He could not sit there and let this girl, who knew so little of life on the frontier, condemn a man who had fought a coward and a bully.

He hitched his chair forward and cleared his throat as if he were preparing to deliver a lecture. 'Miss Broomfield, I'd like to tell you a story about this man you call a beast. I should not do so except that I know what I tell you will be treated with confidence. I attended to Glenister's injuries.'

'Were they serious?' Broomfield asked anxiously.

'No. But the exertion and the terrific beating he received opened up that gunshot wound in his shoulder that he got in the showdown with that outlaw Harper. While I was redressing that wound, he asked about Donovan. I told him that I wasn't sure whether he'd got a fractured skull or not. That perhaps he might have to go to a city hospital back East. Well, Glenister told me to go ahead — that he'd meet any expenses that were incurred.

'Later on he called and told me to consult anyone I wished, regardless of the cost. And that's a man who came into the town as a complete stranger a few months ago and who'd never seen the Donovans before in his life. He was returning the kindness they showed him when they gave him shelter after his fight with the Harper gang.'

As she listened to the story Elizabeth felt uncomfortable. She didn't want to hear any more — she didn't want to be forced to change her opinion and yet she was compelled to listen. She'd hear what the doc had to say. Whatever it was he couldn't compel her to change her views.

The story went on. 'Glenister shed his gun because the mule skinner wasn't toting one — so he could meet him on equal terms. When I came West, twenty-five years ago, I thought the same as you do, Miss Elizabeth, that I'd come amongst barbarians. But today I wouldn't change places with any doctor you could name in the East.'

Broomfield had got up and walked over to the window while the doc had been talking. He turned round abruptly. 'Damn it, Manners, where's Glenister now? You'll not spend a cent of his money on Donovan. The Company'll pay for all his medical treatment. If they won't, I will.'

The girl made no comment. She got up from the table and excused herself. She realized what a mistake she had made. What was worse, she had returned his gift of the silver fox furs. Returned them without a note or explanation.

Glenister had just made the train as she was pulling out. The Donovan affair had caused little excitement among the workers — a fight was a common occurrence. But now that Glenister, who had become a public figure, had taken part and had used his fists and not a gun, the matter had assumed a different complexion.

As he pushed his way through the crowded car congratulations were showered on him from all sides. It was the last thing he wanted. He still ached all over and the interview with the law men had just about shattered his nerves to hell. The only thing he wanted was quiet. He sought refuge with the brakesman.

The man looked up as Glen approached through the car. 'Hyer, Glen. I wore aiming ter look yer up. The big boss's daughter give me this 'ere parcel fer yer.'

The sight of the package was enough. So she had returned the skins. Ah well, mebbe Annie was right. But his feelings were hurt — badly hurt. It all seemed so unfair. Oh well, he'd give them to good old Annie — she wouldn't refuse a gift. What a good sort she really was — he owed her a lot.

Back in camp after a week's rest, he got busy on the many chores that waited for him. He wanted to build a new corral, but the ground was still too hard — he'd have to leave that for a bit longer. Equipment was having a general overhaul in anticipation of the spring thaw. The key men were just raring to go. Among the ordinary workers, however, there was growing discontent. The flowery pictures that the railroad recruiting agents had painted to the emigrants, were not materializing. No work — no pay, was the company's rule. But in order to keep the gangs together and so that they should not starve, food was provided. Its cost would be set off against their future earnings. This arrangement was not so hard on the old hands. They had earned big money in the good weather. More money than they had ever seen before in their lives and, like other workers in seasonable jobs, they had put by for the winter.

It was the newcomers and those who had squandered their wages who were the greatest grumblers. And certainly conditions for some of them were appalling. A bunch of these folk had taken over the old shack mining town of Rich Bar. It was like any one of the many 'ghost towns' of the West. As the diggings had become exhausted the miners had left the place just as it stood — not even troubling to remove their bits of furniture.

It stood on the middle fork of the Feather River and, as its name implied, was a bar of that river in which the 'forty-niners' had found heavy deposits of gold. Rumour had it that more than fourteen million dollars' worth had been found. So rich was every claim that their size was limited to an area of ten square feet.

The derelict saloon still showed traces of its former garish grandeur. Some of its red plush seating had become a nesting place for chickadees and chipmunks and other wild things. The ornate brass work around the bar was green with verdigris. The place was musty with the smell of dust and damp.

More than once as he had stood in its solitude, Glen had wondered what tales of the boom days the thick wooden walls could tell. From the first he had had sympathy with these bohunks who'd had the guts to make their homes among the ricketty shanties.

He had always seen to it that they had their full quota of cows for beef and when he had been out hunting, he had never forgotten to leave them a few jack rabbits, a few duck or an odd deer — anything that would supplement their chuck ration.

These folk had real pioneer blood in their veins and under the leadership of an old-timer by the name of Cooper, they were beginning to find their feet. But as the railroad went forward they would have to follow.

Ten days after his return from Keedie

Glen and two of his riders had driven a dozen steers to Rich Bar. There were signs that the thaw was not far off. Wild geese were already on the move, the thickets resounded to the early song of red-winged blackbirds and blue jays. Foxes, gophers, jack rabbits and even sage hens were beginning to make tracks on the snow. They were aware of the approach of spring.

The river was still frozen, but on the places where the wintry sun had caught it, the ice had the wet look that spoke of an early break-up. As Glen and his riders came into the town there was an unusual silence. Generally a whole tribe of kids had turned out to greet them. Today there was not one to be seen.

Suddenly Glen became aware of a babble of voices coming from behind a bunch of derelict cabins. Leaving the riders to look after the stock, he rode over to investigate. As he drew closer the sound of the excited voices increased. He saw, grovelling among the snow and the debris of years, the entire community.

He drew rein and looked down at them from Rocky's back. Like a bunch of shamefaced children caught in the act, they stood with sheepish grins on their faces and looked at him.

'Howdy,' he drawled. 'What yer doing — skunk-hunting?'

The old-timer Cooper came forward. His fist was tight-clenched, he clutched something.

'Howdy, Glenister. I reckon yer've bin a mighty good friend to us folk. So I'm figgerin' we kin tell yer.' He opened his fist and held out his hand. There, in his horny palm, was a nugget — a gold nugget the size of a pigeon's egg.

'A bunch of the kids had made them a fire in one of the old cabins. I reckon the heat thawed out the ground. One of 'em seed the nugget a-glitterin'.'

Glen reached down and took the nugget. It was gold all right. He handed it back. The others, who had gathered near, stood round in silence.

'I guess it's gold all right, Cooper. But what yer figgering on — that yer've made another strike?'

The old-timer shook his head. 'I guess that'd be too good to be true. But if them forty-niners missed one nugget, mebbe they missed others.'

'There's right good sense in that. But it ain't no good you folks getting notions into yer heads that yer going to be rich 'cos yer found one nugget. Mebbe it wore dropped by one o' the lucky diggers. Rumour had it there wore millions o' dollars o' gold taken out of this ground. 'Tain't likely them old-timers would overlook a big strike. Still, I'm figgering if you fellas want something ter do till work starts again, yer could thaw out the ground hereabouts by lighting fires. Mebbe yer could find enough colour ter pay fer yer baccy.'

'That ain't a bad notion o' yourn, Glenister. What say, fellas, shall we give it a try?' He turned to the bystanders.

'Shore — shore,' came in chorus.

Glen laughed. They were like a bunch of kids. 'Have it yer own way. But don't blame me if yer do a lot o' digging fer naught. Right now I gotta dozen cows fer yer. Come on and take 'em off my hands.'

'That's good news. We wore nigh outa beef. I reckon us folks gotta lot to thankee fer.' Cooper came forward.

Rocky was showing signs of unfriendliness. 'Keep outa the way of old Rocky's hoofs,' Glen advised. 'He's not feeling at all friendly this morning. I figger he scents the thaw a-coming.'

Glenister handed over the cows and after a cup of coffee he and his riders pushed on. Grainger had asked him to see how deep the drifts were beyond Rich Bar.

A week later news came to camp. He had been wrong — it was no isolated nugget. They had made a strike. There, on the very spot on which the old-timers had built their cabins, large quantities of gold were being found in every shovelful of thawed-out gravel.

The news spread like wildfire. The mad rush started. The families, who'd spent the winter half starved in the old cabins, were probably sitting on thousands of dollars' worth of gold.

With this news came the break-up. The thaw was on. The melting snow and ice turned streams into rivers. A trickle became a torrent. Water courses changed their location in a night. Trestle bridges which had taken the engineers months to build, were washed away. The hardfrozen ground was knee deep in slush and mud.

But it was not the thaw that brought work on the railroad to a standstill. It was the gold strike at Rich Bar. Men downed everything — grabbed picks and shovels and headed for the diggings. They came on foot, by wagon, on horse-back. Not only did the W.P. lose its workers. Those of the C.P. in America River Valley, too, converged on the ghost town of Rich Bar.

Excitement reached its height when an Irishman by the name of Mullins got two thousand, nine hundred dollars' worth of gold out of two pans of gravel from his cabin.

With the gold-fever stricken seekers came the riff-raff. Within two weeks Annie had a temporary saloon going at full blast. Whiskey was selling at a dollar a drink. Every known form of gambling was played night and day. Cabin after cabin was pulled down. The lucky ones who had been in possession got thousands of dollars for the old timbers which were re-erected elsewhere.

It was the old story of the gold strikes — the lucky ones got fortunes. But those who really came out on top were the men who had something to sell. Foodstuffs fetched enormous prices. A meal — when you could get it — cost two bucks.

Men hewed and shovelled and then waded into the icy water with their pans, shaking them vigorously till all the muck was gone and only the big stuff remained. Gold, being heaviest of all, would be at the bottom. The first sight of colour would send a man mad.

As the crowd grew — and each day found more arriving, they would move off into the old diggings and from the first it was obvious that the old forty-niners had not missed much.

The claims that were paying were those on the particular piece of ground on which the town had been built. From one claim, right on the old main street, two men took out five thousand dollars' worth of gold in four days.

It seemed that the old prospectors had stuck their cabins on the most convenient spot and had forgotten to pan the gravel beneath them. Small spots of colour were located round and about, but it was from the claims on the site of the old town that gold in any quantity was being found.

Back in the railroad camp Grainger cursed and fumed. But it was of no avail, for the key men of the entire outfit had gone gold mad. Mule teams and engines alike stood idle. There was no one to drive them. Broomfield himself arrived, but there was nothing he could do.

Glen was just on the verge of leaving with a couple of rod and transit men to survey a canyon on the high ground. He got a message that the big boss wanted to see him. He hoped he would not run into Elizabeth, but it was a chance he had to take.

He found all the bosses assembled with Broomfield at the head of the table. The Chief looked even more haggard and ill than the last time that Glen had seen him.

He looked up from the table as Glen entered the room. 'Glenister, I've sent for you because I consider that you know more about this country than any other man on the pay-roll. Take a seat, man. Don't stand. The position is this — this gold strike is costing us thousands of dollars a day. I've never seen this location. What's your personal opinion about it?'

Glen was amazed. What did this fella think he was — a prospector or a mining engineer? He hesitated before answering.

'I'm no mining man. But I've seen these old diggings afore. This is the first I've ever known of where the old-timers have overlooked aught. There's no doubt about it — they have this time. There's gold there — a heap of it. But it's only in one spot. Those that's coming in now ain't got no chance o' finding colour. I'm figgering there's naught left in the old diggings and those are all that's left for 'em. That way I reckon it won't be long afore they'll be back here asking fer their old jobs back again.'

'That, at least, is a ray of hope,' said Broomfield. 'But how long's that going to be?'

Glen shrugged. 'Yer guess is as good as mine.'

Broomfield made a gesture of impatience. 'But don't you understand, Glenister, the company can't stand this drain? We estimate that with the damage that has been done by the storms, floods and such-like, we're back to where we were last summer. We have just got to curtail our expenditure or we shall be broke and all our past work will have been for nothing.'

Glen felt sorry for the Chief. There was no doubt that he was a sick man. He was up against tremendous odds. 'I can't tell yer how yer can get these bohunks back. But I kin tell yer how yer can reduce yer overheads and mebbe make some money.'

Broomfield stared at him — what could he mean? 'How, man?' he asked.

'By using the construction trains to freight in stores from Keedie and other places and using the mule trains to take the stores to the diggings.'

'Darn it, Glenister, I'm not a store-keeper. I'm an engineer.'

Glen shrugged. 'Have yer any idea, boss, what a sack of flour's fetching in the diggings?'

'Not the faintest.'

'Well, it's fetching twenty dollars. It's the same with everything in the way of foodstuff. Yer got the locomotives and the freight cars doing nothing. Yer could haul in enough supplies, by buying in the towns, to pay all yer overheads.'

Grainger had listened in silence to all Glen had had to say.

'He's got something there, Chief. Why, we could use our own stocks immediately and send back for replacements.'

Broomfield was not entirely convinced. 'But that would be helping the gold strike.'

Lyttleton agreed with him. 'If they're without food they'll have to quit.'

Glenister shook his head. 'That's where yer wrong. Mebbe them that ain't struck it rich will. But not them that's making it pay. They'll go on digging. There's another thing I ain't mentioned. Have yer thought what it's going ter be like hauling stores up there in wagons? But across them two canyons yer bridged, its only six miles from here. Then there's my beef contracts. I've bought mor'n three thousand head. Yer can't go back on yer contracts now and I've arranged fer them to come in at two-weekly intervals. Yer kin get treble the price we bought 'em at, over in the diggings.'

Something like a wan smile showed on Broomfield's tired face. 'Well, fellas, I think Glenister has shown us a temporary way of keeping down our costs. I, for one, am darned grateful to him. I hate to think what our backers in 'Frisco would say if they thought we'd become wholesale merchants. But I'm thinking they wouldn't mind so much so long as we reduce our overheads. Go to it, Lyttleton. Grainger and I are returning to 'Frisco to acquaint the stock-holders with some of the difficulties that face us up here. But we shan't be away long and I hope when we get back things will be better. And, Lyttleton, I should give Glenister a free hand. He seems more versed in these matters than we are.'

The meeting broke up and that night Glen watched the Chief's car attached to a locomotive and steam out. Elizabeth Broomfield was aboard. Mebbe she would not return. He felt lonesome at her going. He was crazy and he knew it. He — a convict on parole! But something had stirred inside him every time he had seen her — even at the thought of seeing her. However, it was no good day-dreaming and Glen got on with the job.

The stores sold as he had predicted they would. The two store-keepers were only too pleased to buy at any price, and before long, as he had foreseen, many of the hungry and sadly disillusioned railroad workers were coming in and asking for their old jobs.

In Rich Bar gold was still pouring out — but only for the lucky ones. Before Broomfield and Grainger had returned work on the track had already re-started.

Lyttleton was delighted. He left the supplying of provisions to Rich Bar in Glen's capable hands. The demand there was falling off, but as the men returned to camp more food was required at headquarters. The prices which they had received surprised him. The amount showed a profit more than sufficient to cover all their overheads.

11

Glen and his riders had just delivered fifty head of cows to the local butcher in Rich Bar. He strolled into Annie's new Saloon. Annie was by no means her usual carefree self. She looked anxious and worried.

'Anything wrong, marm?' he asked.

She nodded. 'I'm a bit worried, Glen. I'm carrying a lot of coin and dust. There's some tough hombres in this town.'

'Well, if that's all that's worrying yer, let me take it into the Bank in Keedie tomorrow. I'm collecting a bunch of cows at Twin Forks and I kin easy break my journey.'

'Would yer, Glen? It'll be a load off my mind.'

'Go get it.' Another couple of drinks and he took his departure. The following day he deposited the coin at the Bank.

Three days later he returned and when he went into Lyttleton's office he was surprised to find Cooper, the old-timer from Rich Bar. Cooper was one of the lucky ones — his claim was among the best on the diggings.

'Hyer, Glen,' Lyttleton greeted him; 'I'm glad you got in. Cooper here's come in to see you.'

'Howdy, Cooper. What's on yer mind?'

'Howdy. I come to see if yer'd do fer us what yer dun fer Railroad Annie.'

Glenister was giving nothing away. 'And what might I have dun fer Annie?'

'Yer took her dust out.'

'Who told yer I took her dust out, Cooper?'

'She did herself. We'd pay yer well.'

'What I dun fer Annie was a personal matter. How much you fellas wanting ter ship out?'

'Nigh on two hundred thousand and there'll be more.'

Lyttleton gasped in amazement. He pursed his lips and whistled.

'Doggorn it, fella. Is this all yer own coin?'

'No. It belongs to the lot of us that made the first strike. There's been some tough hombres around lately and they ain't miners.'

'Why can't yer take it yerself?' Glen asked him.

'We darn't leave the diggings fer claim jumpers.'

Glen shook his head. 'Sorry, Cooper. It's too much of a responsibility.'

'I'm telling yer, Glenister, we'd pay yer well.'

'It's no use fella. Besides, I'm employed by the railroad. I'm not my own boss.'

As the two men talked Lyttleton had been looking from one to the other. This might mean business for the railroad. 'You say there's more to be shipped?' he asked.

'Yes. The other fellas want to get their's out, too.'

'How much are you prepared to pay?' Glenister looked at him in surprise.

228

Cooper hesitated. 'I'll tell you what I have in mind,' Lyttleton continued. 'The company could take this out for you if it was a regular shipment. But if we'd got to send men over to the diggings and then take it up to Keedie, the rate would be high. It would be cheaper if you brought the dust here yourselves.'

'We'll have it here afore sun-down tomorrow,' Cooper promised.

'I'm warning you the rate will be high,' said Lyttleton.

'We shan't mind that as long as its outa our cabins. Thankee.'

'All right,' Lyttleton agreed. 'A regular weekly shipment will show a good return. All we'll have to do is to put a guard on the car that's carrying it. Besides — who's to know?'

Glen did not like the idea. It was not his business, but all the same he felt that Lyttleton was taking a risk.

'I don't like it,' he said. 'If there was an organized service like south of Keedie it would be different. Supposing there was a slip-up, whose responsibility would it be? I know what the folks in Rich Bar'd think — the Railroad's.'

'All right, Glen. The responsibility will be mine. I know shipments of this sort at one per cent should show the company a darn good profit.'

Glen shrugged his shoulders. 'Have it yer own way, fella. It ain't none o' my business. But if I wore you I'd see I had some of them tough bohunks around. Well, so long, Cooper. I'll be seeing yer.'

He left the two men talking. Running the railroad was not his business. If Lyttleton wanted to take such a risk it was up to him. But he couldn't help wondering if Broomfield would have agreed to such a proposition. Two hundred thousand was a mighty big heap of coin and with the gang of rough-necks he'd seen hanging around Rich Bar, anything might happen.

For the next couple of days he and his hands were busy on the new corral. He'd got more than seven thousand head out on the range and the animals were brought in for slaughter as they were required.

It was well on into the afternoon when their attention was attracted to one of the locos. She was whistling like mad and coming at a hell of a bat. But after a passing glance at her, they took no further notice.

Ten minutes later one of Lyttleton's assistants rushed up out of breath — would Glenister please come at once. Mr. Lyttleton wanted him.

Glen downed tools and followed. He found Lyttleton pacing from end to end of his cabin. The engineer and a conductor stood by the table. Their faces were white and drawn.

Lyttleton lost no time. 'The Harper gang stuck-up the train — shot the brakesman and the guard and got away with the gold. Darn yer, Glenister, say something. But for the Lord's sake don't tell me you warned me.'

Glen looked at the engineer. 'Where'd this happen and how d'yer know it wore the Harper gang?'

'It happened between fifty-one and forty-nine section. They'd ripped about thirty yards of rail up. I had to stop. When I did, they boarded us. Charlie and the guard put up the hell of a fight, but they blew the car open with dynamite. As they were leaving, the leader, a big fella, said, 'Tell them bosses o' yourn this'll pay for the cows.''

'How many of them wore there?'

'I should say nigh on a dozen.'

Glen turned to Lyttleton — there wasn't any time to lose; 'Can yer get a repair gang right away to put them rails down?' He felt sorry for him — this might mean his job.

'Shore. What you aiming to do?'

'We gotta get a posse together. I want an engine with a coupla cars — mebbe three. I'm playing a hunch this gang's got a hide-out somewhere round Twin Forks. If I'm right we might be able to head them off. But we gotta have some of the posse that kin ride and shoot. We kin stop at Keedie and get the sheriff.'

'I'll get things moving and I'm coming with you.'

'No. You stay here and see things are all right this end. I'll do my best to get yer back the coin. Yer'll have to cope with the Rich Bar crowd if they come over. I'm a-figgering it won't be long afore them diggers are a-hollering their heads off. Tell 'em I've gone after the gang. It'll mebbe keep 'em quiet a while.'

He collected his own three hands and another four of the technical staff who could handle a gun. By the time they were ready, a loco with steam up was waiting for them.

They got the horses aboard and Glenister told the engineer to let her roll. They were delayed for an hour at the scene of the hold-up. The work team had not got the line completely relaid.

Glen made use of the opportunity to do a bit of sign reading. There had been a dozen in that gang all right and their tracks headed east. Foot by foot he combed the ground. It was as he had thought. If their hide-out was in the foothills around Twin Forks, they'd have had to go east or west and then turn north to miss Keedie. The tracks told him nothing except that one horse had lost a shoe.

Though he still had nothing definite to go on, his hunch made him determined to try the Twin Fork country. He estimated that the gang had from four to five hours' lead. By using the train and with only a quick stop at Keedie to pick up the sheriff and his posse, Glen hoped to hit Twin Forks Junction before midnight. If his brother Roy was the leader, Glen knew there'd be no share-out of the gold before they got back to their hide-out.

From what the two lawmen from Carson and Salt Lake had said, he was convinced that Sarah was the brains of the outfit. It was just the sort of thing she'd love. He could imagine her

— with her green eyes glinting, planning and scheming every move.

The gang must have had someone on the look-out in Rich Bar the whole time. News of the discovery of gold would act like a magnet and knowing that he was working for the railroad that was freighting the gold, it would please that low cunning nature of hers to get one back at him in revenge for the cows they had lost.

He was sure he was right. Why, otherwise, would the leader have been fool enough to mention cows to the engineer? It was just the loco sort of thing that Roy would do.

The only thing he could not understand was how they knew which train was carrying the gold. Possibly someone in Cooper's party had opened his mouth too wide.

Glen had been prepared to let his brother Roy go his own way, so long as he did not interfere with his life. But the fact that he was a McCreedie would make folks connect them and before he knew where he was there'd be a repetition of what had happened previously, he would be suspected although he was perfectly innocent.

He liked his job with the railroad. For the first time in his life he was trusted and no longer pointed out as the son of an outlaw.

No doubt the fact of his relationship to Roy would become known. Oh, well, even if Broomfield kicked him out, he would have done his job.

He knew that Roy would never give up the owl-hoot while he had Sarah tagging along with him to egg him on. She had been the evil genius all through. The love that he'd once had for her had turned to hate during the years he had spent in Rocky Point.

He walked back to the track. The rails had been laid in position and without further delay, they were off. When they got to Keedie they were lucky enough to find Sheriff Taylor in his office.

As soon as he heard Glen's story he

gave orders for a posse to be got together right away. Glen told him of his hunch about Twin Forks, but at first he did not agree. He was for heading back to the scene of the hold-up and taking up the trail from that spot.

'What makes yer think he'll head fer that country?' he asked Glen.

''Cos them cows I took from 'em had not come far. In the first place, with the snow as thick as it wore, they couldn't have got through. And secondly, them dogies worn't in no shape to do any travelling. Somewhere in them parts the gang's got a hide-out big enough to hold stock. The owners told me they only lost 'em in ones and twos or they'd have been missed sooner.'

Glen took a big breath — it was bound to come out sooner or later. He'd get it over with. 'Finally, I know the gang's new leader.'

The sheriff had been seeing to his guns. He stopped and looked up. 'Yer know the boss of the gang?'

'I should do — he's my brother.'

At first the sheriff's face was one of amazement. Now it became grim. 'Just what are yer handing me out, Glenister?'

'My full name, Taylor, is John Glenister McCreedie. If I'm not mistaken the leader of the Harper gang is my younger brother, Roy McCreedie. I came across him in that fracas we had over the cows.'

The sheriff had sat down, but he had never taken his eyes from Glen's face.

'McCreedie,' he repeated thoughtfully. 'Clinton McCreedie. So that tough old owl-hooter was yer paw, I'm figgering. They always said he had a wife and a coupla brats tucked away in the hills. That shore explains a lot — but not all. Are yer aiming ter tell me the rest?'

Glen hitched himself on to the corner of the table and pushed his hat to the back of his head. 'I guess I might as well get it off my chest ter someone. I've had it bottled up too long. Roy's a year younger than me and all my life

I've seemed to be taking the blame fer him. Four years ago he stuck up a Bank in Ogden. I worn't within twenty miles of the place that day, but they picked me up and seeing we're so much alike, they identified me as him. I got ten years in spite of swearing I worn't there.'

Taylor had listened without any comment.

Glen took the makings from his pocket and rolled himself a cigarette. He lit it and blew a cloud of smoke into the air. Then he went on: 'When I come up here I'd just been granted parole after serving three of 'em. I was aiming to get right away, but of all the blame luck the Harper gang had to pick on the train I was travelling on. But it worn't till the fracas over the cows that I realized Roy was one of that gang. And that worn't till he had me covered and I'd been plugged in the shoulder. I ain't taking no more.' He got down from the table and walked across the office and back again.

'When it becomes known he's my kin mebbe it'll cost me my job with the railroad.'

The sheriff got to his feet and stuck out his hand. 'Shake, fella. I, fer one, am with yer.'

Glen took the proffered hand and that shake was to seal a friendship that lasted a lifetime. 'I reckon yer had a raw deal and I shouldn't worry about losing yer job. From what I hear Broomfield thinks a heap of yer and there's a good many friends o' yourn right here in the town. If this brother looks so like yer, it's as well yer told me. It may save any trouble in the future. Come on — we'll head fer Twin Forks as yer said.'

They reached the junction during the night and so that they might escape notice, Glen had the engineer pull on to the loop and damp down his fires. They unloaded the horses and pushed off.

For two days and nights they combed the country without seeing hide or hair of any of the gang. They had decided to give up the search and had already headed towards the junction. As they stopped to water their mounts in a thickly wooded draw the sheriff thought he caught the sound of a shod hoof on rock.

Bidding the posse keep quiet and hold the mounts' muzzles in case they whinnied, he and Glenister pushed their way through the aspen thicket. Not two hundred yards away and heading for the same draw, was a bunch of riders.

Glen whispered, 'It's them — the Harper gang.'

Within seconds he and the sheriff were back with the posse. Quickly explaining the position, the sheriff ordered them to scatter and take cover.

'Remember,' he whispered, 'we want 'em alive if possible. But don't take any chances.'

The gang were in high spirits. They came riding along without the slightest suspicion of danger. At their head rode Roy McCreedie and by his side, a slim figure. It was this figure that held all

Glen's attention. There was no mistaking it in spite of the range rider's duds. It was Sarah. Sarah with the beautiful sun-tanned face, delicately moulded nose and vivacious mouth. From where Glen stood he could not see her eyes, but an unruly lock of black hair showed from under her white sombrero.

Her shapely figure was clad in a pale blue shirt — she wore a loosely knotted crimson bandanna round her slender neck. Glen's mind went back to the times in Rocky Point when he had wanted to put his strong sinewy hands around that neck and he shuddered.

The pearl-inlaid butt of a ·45 showed from a holster attached to a belt around her waist. That gun was no toy. Many a time he had seen her shoot the pips on a playing-card. Her draw was faster than most men's. She was laughing at some remark of Roy's when one of the posse's mounts whinnied.

The outlaws dived for their guns, but they never had a chance.

Glen heard his brother yell to her,

'Ride fer it. We're ambushed.' He saw Roy spur to the front in the hope of protecting her. Then the sheriff's voice boomed out:

'Drop yer guns, fellas. Yer ain't gotta chance. We got yer covered from all sides.'

The gang fired blindly into the brush. A blast from the posse emptied five saddles. Panic-stricken horses and men scattered for cover — their position was hopeless.

Glen saw Sarah spin her mount around and tear off back on the way they had come. Roy's guns blasted at the unseen foe. It was only a matter of time before he would stop a bullet.

Glen had not yet fired — he would hate to see his brother die. His gun roared. Roy's mount dropped under him.

'Yer ain't gotta chance, Roy. Throw down yer guns,' he shouted.

Sarah and one of the outlaws were making their getaway. Bullets hummed all round them. Either the shooting was bad, or they bore charmed lives, for they still kept going. The rest of the gang had had enough, their hands were up.

As Roy gathered himself from the ground he dropped his guns and he, too, hoisted his hands in sign of surrender.

'It ain't no use, fellas,' Glen heard him say. 'We ain't gotta chance.'

Glenister and the sheriff pushed their way through the thicket and confronted him.

As Roy saw his brother he grinned. 'I mighta knowed yer had a hand in it. How'd yer figger we come this way — or was it just luck?'

'I warned yer last time we met, Roy, to quit this game. I ain't no law officer. But when yer interfered with the property of the railroad I took a hand.'

Roy laughed sarcastically. 'You a lawman! It ain't going ter do yer no good when folks realize what yer are ter me.'

The posse stood with drawn guns

eyeing the two brothers. There was little wonder for side by side they were as alike as two peas.

'Cut the cackle!' snapped the sheriff. He was anxious to save Glen from further embarrassment. 'Get their hardware and put a rope on the galoots. Where's the gold?' he asked Roy.

'Yer'll find it on that spare bronc yonder. When kin I put my arms down? I'm figgering we're all getting tired.'

'See they got no guns hidden,' the sheriff told the posse.

They found the gold intact. Taylor was determined to take no chances with a gang of such desperate characters — each man's hands were securely bound.

As soon as this was completed they headed for the junction and the waiting train. The sheriff was delighted with the capture. The Harper gang were famous and their round-up would be a feather in his cap and he had not forgotten that several of them had a price on their heads. The dead were loaded on to their mounts and the cavalcade started on their journey.

Glen rode in silence in the rear. Taylor drew alongside. 'Well, Glen, yer hunch was right. I reckon this is a mighty good day's work. Pity them other two got away, but I guess they'll high tail it to other parts and that won't be my worry. I'm figgering that there brother o' yourn aims to make things a mite unpleasant fer yer.'

Glenister looked grim. 'It can't be helped. It was bound to come out some time or other. I dun my part by the railroad. If they don't take kindly to having a jail bird working for 'em, I kin push off.'

The sheriff looked at the grim face. It was sure hard on this fella. He hoped it would work out all right. 'Nary yer have any fears. The fact they got the coin and the dust back'll be enough. I intend to make it clear that the whole idea of coming down here was yourn. To go against yer own blood shore takes guts. I'm handing it ter yer.'

'That's what I feels so bad about, sheriff. If the judge only sends him to the Pen I'm hoping it will knock some sense into that conceited thick skull of his. Before he's allus let other folks pay for his crimes. But supposing they hangs him? There's a lot o' fella's deaths chalked up against this gang. Didn't they kill a Bank teller in Virginia City?'

Sheriff Taylor looked at him curiously — what was he getting at?

'Yer ain't got any fool notions o' letting him go, have yer?'

'Nary talk so loco, Taylor. Would I have gone ter all this trouble just ter let him go again?'

'Yer might — now yer got the gold back. I shore appreciate how yer feel — him being yer brother. But I'm warning yer, Glen, let him take his chance with the others and stand his trial same as them.'

Though there had been no actual threat in Taylor's remarks Glen knew what he meant.

When they got the prisoners safely aboard the train and on their way to Keedie, Roy started to get unpleasant. On their way in he had joked and treated the capture as just a bit of bad luck.

The whole gang seemed in good spirits in spite of the deaths of their pards. Taylor was feeling uneasy. He never took his eyes off the two brothers. He did not actually distrust Glen, but he was a good judge of men and he knew what Glenister must be going through in his mind. If the worst did occur and Roy were sentenced to death, Glen would know that folks would point him out as the man who had sent his own brother to the gallows.

He was deep in these thoughts when Roy began to pick on his brother. 'What you fellas say to a fella that turns his own brother over to the law?' he asked the posse.

Their eyes turned to Glenister. They had not known of the relationship, but the resemblance of the two men set them wondering.

One of the gang replied, 'A fella that would do that's lower than a skunk, I'm thinking.'

'Well, the great railroad man over there is my brother, Glenister McCreedie. Take a good look at him, fellas — all fer a few lousy dollars!'

Glen's face was scarlet. He was seething with anger. He would have liked to smash that sneering grin off his brother's face. But he bit his tongue and remained silent.

Roy went on with his baiting. 'The ex-convict from Rocky Point — the ex-bank robber now turned beef buyer for the railroad.'

The men of the posse looked at one another. Glenister an ex-convict!

Glen could see from their faces what they were thinking. The sheriff came to his rescue. 'McCreedie,' he said through tight lips, 'yer paw may have been an outlaw, but at least he was a man. Yer nothing but a lying skunk. Glenister here doesn't say a word, but

I'm figgering he thinks a lot. Probably he thinks the same as I would — that he's ashamed yer bear the same name as he does. Go on, tell 'em why he's an ex-convict. Tell 'em that it wore you held up the Bank in Ogden. And that because unfortunately he looks like you, they pinned it on him while you slunk in the hills.'

There was a stir among the posse. Some leaned forward as if to listen more intently. Glen's own riders shuffled their feet. The whole atmosphere was tense and uncomfortable.

Roy was silent. He tried to put on an air of bravado and laughed in a forced way.

The sheriff had not finished with him. 'He took the rap fer you becos' yer wore his kid brother. When he got his parole yer still hung on to his shirt, figgering he'd cover yer up. He told yer ter quit when he tangled with Harper. Yer grabbed this gold figgering he'd do naught about it. Fer once yer wore wrong. Glen's stood all he's going ter stand from a skunk like you.'

Roy McCreedie had recovered some of his blustering manner. He laughed scornfully. 'So that's the tale he's told yer, is it? Records don't lie. It wore him got ten years fer that Bank job — not me. As fer the rumpus over the cows — I could have put a slug into him, but he begged fer his life.'

So far the argument had been left to the sheriff, but this last remark of Roy's was too much for Glen's riders. 'Yer a blame liar, Roy McCreedie,' said one of them; 'I wore there. You and them skunks o' yourn outnumbered us by three to one. And the boss had a slug in him after beating Harper to the draw. Yer high-tailed it when yer seed the train crew wore a-coming with their rifles. Us fellas that's worked with him, knows him. And I, fer one, am pleased to call him my pard and my boss.'

'And me,' 'And me,' came a chorus.

'Thanks, fellas,' said Glen quietly; 'I'm shore grateful.'

He turned to his brother. Roy's face

was a mask of hate.

'Yer see, Roy, folks are judged by their actions — not by words. If yer hands hadn't been tied I'd have pushed yer lies down yer throat. I warned yer afore ter quit. Yer didn't take the warning. I may lose my job with the railroad when they know I'm a kin ter you. But I got the satisfaction of knowing I had a hand in getting the dust back fer them folks that's sweated their souls out digging fer it. I'm hoping the Pen will do what Maw nor me could ever do — that's make a man out of yer.'

'The Pen!' scoffed Roy. 'There ain't no jail will hold me, not the Pen neither.'

Glenister grinned for the first time. 'Mebbe yer'll change yer mind.'

This was too much for Roy. In spite of his tied hands, he hurled himself at his brother.

Glen met him with a straight right to the chin. He dropped like a log. Glen casually dusted his knuckles. 'I reckon we might have some peace now.'

The remark brought a laugh from the posse. The other members of the Harper gang cursed. They made no attempt to help their prostrate leader. And there were no more words from the sullen Roy when, eventually, he came to.

12

News of the capture of the Harper gang caused a sensation throughout three States. The papers featured the fact that John Glenister was the brother of the gang's leader under the headline — 'THIS HUMAN DRAMA'.

The editor of the *Epitaph* excelled himself. Inch-high type proclaimed — 'LOYALTY STRONGER THAN BLOOD'. The leader writer really let himself go:

By the capture of the dreaded Harper Gang a human drama, stranger than any conception of a fiction writer, has been revealed.

The gang have terrorized the States of California, Nevada and Utah for the past three years. Here, in the border town of Keedie, an amazing story has reached its climax. Clinton McCreedie, an old-time gunman of the owl-hoot, had two sons — Glenister and Roy. The former, the elder of the boys, hated all forms of lawlessness and craved for the life of an honest citizen. Roy followed in the footsteps of the father. The lonely trail of the badlands, the roar of a gun, the whistle of a bullet, and the smell of cordite were his life. He had never known any other.

Glenister, up in his cabin at the camp, threw the paper away in disgust. He had no wish to read any more. This was the end. Every paper from here to the coast would be full of the miserable story. In a matter of hours they would be on his trail from Salt Lake City for the killing of Gorman.

He began to collect his possessions. He was strapping up his bedroll when the cabin door opened. Lyttleton came in.

'Hyer, Glen. Going some place?'

'I figger so. I guess it was time I was

drifting. I aim to beat the old man firing me.'

Lyttleton stared at him. 'What in 'tarnation are you talking about? Why, the whole camp's talking about what you done and I hear the folks over at Rich Bar intend to give you a presentation. As for beating the old man — he's here already and bellowing for you like a mad bull. I've come to fetch you. It's me that nearly got fired for agreeing to freight in that darn gold dust. But now they seen our profit on the food deal, their curses have turned to blessings.' He laughed. 'I tell you, you and me are tops at the moment.'

Glen got up from the floor where he'd been fixing his bedroll. This sounded all right — but had they seen the papers?

'What about all that bunk in the paper there?' He pointed to a corner of the cabin where he had thrown the news-sheet.

'That?' said Lyttleton. 'Why, we all think you had a pretty raw deal.

Broomfield's talking about seeing the Governor about a free pardon. This brother of yours must be a hell of a hog.'

Glenister tried to think. Things were getting worse instead of better. The Governor of the State now and a free pardon! He knew what that 'free pardon' would be. No — nothing would get him over the State Line into Utah. He'd better go and bluff it out and then high tail it at the first opportunity. Besides, there was Elizabeth.

'Is she with him?' he asked.

Lyttleton looked surprised. 'Elizabeth? Shore. She was lapping up your life story in the *Epitaph* when I left.'

So she knew as well. All right, he'd go and get it over with.

'Come on, yer crazy galoot. I reckon I gotta thank you fer getting me in this mess.' He picked up his hat and headed for the siding.

Lyttleton followed him. 'I like that. I get you a rise in pay and you call me names!'

Broomfield and Grainger were waiting for them.

Glen clambered into the Chief's car. 'Howdy, boss.'

'Howdy. Sit down — the pair of you. You seem to have been having some excitement in my absence, Glenister.'

'Mor'n I like, boss.'

The Chief smiled. 'Well, Mr. Grainger and I are both delighted with the progress that's been made. You've both done a good job of work. But about this other matter.'

Glenister's heart sank — here it came. Broomfield was still talking as if things were all right — perhaps they were.

'I am appalled at the injustice you have suffered. I intend to see that you get full restitution. This brother of yours must be an utter blackguard. I congratulate you on your courage in going after him and securing the return of the stolen property. A claim against us for two hundred thousand dollars at this stage would just about have finished us when the stock-holders heard of it. The responsibility for such freight on a construction train should never have been accepted.'

For a moment Broomfield looked severely at Lyttleton. Then he smiled. 'However, we won't go into that any further. Lyttleton already knows my views on the matter and Mr. Grainger agrees with me. We intend to recognize your services. Your pay is increased to a thousand dollars a month.'

Glen stared at him. He could hardly believe his ears.

'That's mighty generous of yer, but — '

Before he could say any more Broomfield interrupted him.

'Don't say any more. You deserve the increase. Go ahead as you've been doing. By the way, you'll be pleased to hear that your friend Donovan is well on the way to recovery. He did not have a fractured skull.'

'That's good news. I reckon his wife'll be mighty pleased.'

As Glen left the car he came face to face with Elizabeth. 'Howdy, marm,' he muttered and stood aside.

'Good afternoon.'

She appeared ill at ease. Glen twiddled the brim of his hat.

'I'm glad to see yer back, marm.'

'I'm glad to be back. Somehow San Francisco did not appear to be the same. I hear you've been having exciting times up here with the gold strike. I'd like to see Rich Bar.'

'Just say when, marm. I'd be mighty proud ter show yer and that mare of yourn could do with a bit of work. She's getting fat.'

'I'll remember,' said Elizabeth and with that she had gone.

Glen walked back to his cabin. He had a lot to think about. He could see no way but to brazen it out. After all, no one here knew about the Gorman affair in Salt Lake City. They had nothing on him and if it came to a show-down, well, then he might run.

Elizabeth had condescended to speak

to him again and they were paying him a mighty lot of coin. If only he were left in peace that spread of his dreams looked like materializing.

If Donovan no longer needed that coin he might use the reward money to make a down payment on a spread he knew of lower down the Feather River. He'd heard the owner wanted to sell. He'd stick it out at least till after Roy's trial. They'd still got him in jail in Keedie.

Glen hadn't been near the town, but rumour had it that the sheriff was taking no chances. A special guard had been put on day and night till the gang were sent south for trial. He felt restless. He couldn't set his mind to anything. He'd ride over to Rich Bar and see Annie. He'd heard that she was selling her saloon and going back to the Line End.

When he got in he found the bar well filled. Congratulations came from all sides. Miners were still pouring into the place in spite of the fact that there had been no big strike. The wise ones were cashing in and getting out.

Annie was in her usual corner. 'Hyer, Glen,' she called as he made his way across the saloon. She took down a bottle and slid it and a glass over to him. 'I'm glad yer showed up. The boys are plumb anxious ter thank yer in mor'n words.'

'That's mighty nice of 'em. But I'd be grateful if they'd let the whole blame business die. What's this I hear about yer selling out?'

'It ain't settled yet. But I'm figgering yer wore right — the gold's soon going to peter out. I cleaned up and I ain't worrying none if I just ups and gets back to Keedie. I've knowed the fella that's dickering ter buy for twenty-five years or more. He's one of these slick grafters who's been around railroads ever since he wore a kid. He figgers that Rich Bar's handy for both construction camps and when the gold's gone the workers'll still want their likker. Mebbe he's right. But I ain't so spry as I used ter be and the Line End'll do me.'

She filled herself a glass of bourbon and took a long drink.

'Listen, Glen. It ain't making the dough that worries me none these days. It's keeping it when yer got it. I had no end of sleepless nights till yer took that coin ter the Bank fer me.'

Glen finished his drink and helped himself to another. 'What made yer so scared? It ain't like yer.'

'I dunno. There wore a shifty-eyed gent hanging around here. I figger he wore that gang's lookout man. The day Cooper and the boys took that boodle over ter the camp, I seed him high-tailing it at a hell of a bat. Now the railroad bosses know who yer are — how are they taking it?'

Glen laughed. 'That's where it's plumb loco. I expected 'em to fire me. Instead they give me a rise.'

Annie snorted. 'So they oughter. I reckon if it hadn't been fer you, things would have been mighty different. Don't tell me it wore Bert Taylor's idea, going ter Twin Forks. I ain't naught against the sheriff. He's a good fella in a tough job. But I ain't figgering on him being too bright.'

The saloon door opened — Annie looked up. 'Here's the fella that's dickering ter buy — coming in now.'

Glen followed her gaze. Coming straight towards them was Big Shot Finney.

He must have started, for Annie said in an undertone, 'Yer know him?'

'Shore.'

Finney was dressed to kill. He looked very different from the last time Glen had seen him. He wore a grey cut-away coat and his pants were pushed into high-legged black boots, polished till they shone. A large diamond glittered in his white shirt and his broad-brimmed black hat was the head-piece usually sported by gamblers.

As he recognized Glen his black piggy eyes lit up. He stuck out a fat podgy hand on which another diamond sparkled. 'Glenister McCreedie by all that's holy! The very guy I've been waiting ter see. How are yer?'

'Howdy, Finney.'

'Big Shot Finney' grinned at Annie.

'Now, Annie, me old darling, set 'em up — the best in the house. This is a special occasion. It ain't often a guy has the pleasure of buying a drink fer the fella that saved his life.'

Annie sniffed. 'Not so much of 'the old darling'. And when did Glenister ever save yer worthless neck?'

'That's another story, me dear.'

Annie poured out the drinks.

'Well here's to yer,' said Finney, picking up his glass and nodding to Glen. 'And you, my queen o' the track.' He downed his drink and wiped his mouth with the back of his hand. 'By all accounts yer've been having a grand time since last we met,' he said to Glen.

Annie had been watching Finney with interest. She didn't like his exaggerated show of friendliness.

'And where was it you two met last?' she asked.

Glen answered. 'In the Pen.'

'So that's where yer've been, Finney. I wondered where yer'd got to. What was it for this time? That woman o' yourn get mad with yer? Or wore yer getting outa the way of a bunch o' yer own countrymen yer'd Shanghai-ed inter the railroads? Mebbe yer don't know it, Glen, but this critter's kidded more immigrants to working on the railroads, with his flowery speeches, than hours yer've lived in the whole of yer life.' She laughed. 'Now he's fancying himself in a saloon. Figgering now he's got the poor suckers up here, he'll take the coin off 'em with bad likker.'

Finney burst into a blustering laugh. Some of Annie's remarks had stung, but he was determined to treat it all as a joke.

'There yer go again, Annie. Yer've been selling rot-gut fer years to these bohunks. Where'd yer be if it weren't fer the likes of me who get yer yer trade? As fer my visit to the Pen — me and the judge didn't see eye to eye on a small matter.'

Annie left the two men together and went off to serve a customer.

Glenister had no wish to waste time — if Finney wanted to see him, the sooner they got their business over the better. 'What wore yer wanting ter see me about, Finney?'

'Come on — let's sit down.' Finney picked up the bottle and glasses and Glen followed him to a table in a corner.

'Fer a guy with only a few bucks in his jeans I gotta hand it ter yer, Glenister. Yer shore landed yerself with a swell job with old Broomfield. That's what I want ter talk about.'

Glen helped himself to another drink and listened carefully as Finney gabbled on. 'The trouble is, Glen, yer joined up with the wrong outfit. The ones yer with ain't got the dough — the others have. I've been around railroads all me life and I'm telling yer I ain't ever seen worse country than this Feather River.

267

This granite is shore going ter be hell on the men. The trouble is there ain't enough of 'em to go round. My dough's on the American River outfit. But I want yer help.'

Glen stared at him — what was he getting at? How could he help?

'Why me?' he asked.

''Cos folk around here think yer a tin gawd. Since I hit this burgh I ain't heard nothing but what a swell guy yer are. I'm shore taking my hat off ter yer, tangling with that brother of yourn. Now see here, that reputation of yourn is worth dough. All yer gotta do is change outfits and give these mugs the spiel and they'll follow yer. I don't care what dough they're paying yer — my folk'll double it.'

Still Glen was silent. Finney was a dirty snake, but he'd listen and see how much further the dirty rat would go.

Finney downed another drink — smacked his lips and continued. 'Yer gotta remember there's a heap o' coin awaiting for the boss that puts steel across them there mountains.' He waved his hand to where the High Sierras gleamed in the setting sun. 'My folks aim ter be first and they'll pay big coin ter them that helps 'em. What yer say?'

'I reckon yer got me wrong, Finney. I'm staying loyal to the folk who've been mighty good ter me. As far as I'm concerned my dough's on us going through the Beckwith Pass first.'

The smile had left Finney's face. His expression was the same that Glenister had come to hate in Rocky Point.

'I'm figgering yer forgetting one thing, McCreedie. There wore a guard called Gorman. The night yer pulled out he wore found with a slug in him outside Mooney's.'

'Gorman,' said Glen; 'Gorman? I remember him. A mean critter that used ter knock poor old Luny about. I guess he had it coming ter him. What's it got ter do with me?'

'Quit stalling, fella,' Finney snarled. 'Yer know blame well it wore your slug that finished him off.'

Glenister laughed in his face. 'That's rich, that is. Who d'yer think yer kidding, fella?'

'Kidding, am I?' Finney scoffed. 'Join up with me or I produce the guy that says yer plugged him. Shall I tell yer how yer did it? Yer saw him playing cards and called him outside. Neither of yer come back. He wore found next morning. Yer never caught the construction train Mooney'd arranged fer yer. Why? 'Cos yer'd plugged him and yer had ter beat it. Yer'd got the two hundred bucks Mooney'd given yer and the roll yer'd won playing crap so yer figgered yer wore all right. Now, fella, talk yerself outa that.'

Glenister's hand hung over his gun. His eyes bored into Finney.

'I'm warning yer, Finney, open yer trap once more and I'll send yer ter hell where I'm figgering yer belong. Yer don't scare me none — yer frame-up don't work.'

'McCreedie, d'yer think I'm loco? If

anything happens ter me, Val Mooney and my attorney knows the facts. Think it over, I'm here to stay. This joint'll be mine tomorrow and I'm figgering I'm on the best thing in my life. It'll be blame funny to have the McCreedie brothers in the dock together.' He got up and walked out.

Glen did not move. He was framed — beautifully framed for the second time in his life. He sat staring at his drink unaware that anyone had joined him. A voice at his elbow brought him out of his black thoughts.

'What's wrong, Glen? What's that ornery, low, two-faced skunk got on yer?' It was Annie.

'I guess he's got me framed.' He told her the whole story.

'Are yer shore this fella Gorman was dead?' she asked.

'Certain as I'm sittin' here.'

'Well then, it's the fella that plugged him that's given Finney the lowdown. Yer say there was no one else around.'

'I'm shore there wasn't.'

'The bullet that got him just missed you?'

'Yeah.'

'Could it have been intended fer you? Supposing the tinhorn yer won the coin off was sore. He'd have it in fer yer. Suppose his bullet got this fella instead of you?' She stopped. Suddenly she clicked her fingers. 'Darn it — what's the matter with me? He's got a tinhorn with him up here. A mean ferritty-eyed critter with a lantern jaw.'

'That's him,' said Glen.

'All right. You leave this ter me. I'm a good hand at smelling out skunks. When the time's right I'll send fer yer. Now, you carry on as if naught's happened.'

'Doggorn it, Annie, am I never ter be outa yer debt?'

'Stow it. Ain't yer dun enough fer me?' she snapped. 'Finney can have this joint — if he's got the coin. And mebbe it won't do him the good he thinks it will. There's only one thing I asks yer — don't go gunning fer 'em.'

'I'll promise yer that if yer promise yer won't go sticking yer neck out on my account.'

'All right. Come on now — let's have a drink and you snap out of it. I've tangled with scum like Big Shot Finney mor'n once in the past and they've never got the better of Railroad Annie.'

Glen downed his drink, set down the glass and got up. 'I shore dunno what ter say when I gotta have a female ter save me neck.'

'Away with yer now. Get yer back ter camp, and remember, keep that iron o' yourn in its holster.'

Glen took her hand in his. 'So long, old-timer. I shan't forget.'

13

Glen rode back into the camp and the following day he went off on a cattle-buying trip.

Elizabeth Broomfield sat alone in the sitting-room of her father's private car. She had read and re-read the story of Glenister McCreedie's life as recorded in the *Epitaph*.

She had misjudged him. Now she understood many of his remarks which had puzzled her. No wonder he loved the freedom of the country after spending three years behind stone walls. She wanted to apologize for having returned his gift of the silver fox furs, but he had given her no opportunity.

She thought of his generosity to the Donovans — of Rocky's love for him and the respect which he had earned among the workers. She wanted to tell him how wrong she knew she had been.

She had never felt this way about any man before. Even when she was in 'Frisco, he had never been out of her thoughts. Surely she was not in love with him? But it was strange that when he was around she felt confident and secure. She would go for a ride and perhaps she would bump into him.

At the horse corral she learnt that he had left camp for a day or two. Lyttleton, too, was away with her father on a survey. She had no wish to ride alone. She went back to the car — threw off her hat and sat down to think.

Suddenly the door behind her opened. She turned and found herself looking into the barrel of a revolver. The hand that held it looked firm and efficient. Her eyes travelled upwards. She looked into the face of the most beautiful woman she had ever seen.

'Don't move,' came a husky voice behind the gun. 'Do as yer told and yer won't get hurt.'

'Who are you and how dare you

come in here uninvited!'

'Cut the cackle, sister. Grab a few things. You and me's taking a trip.'

'I certainly am not.' Elizabeth was frightened — but she was not going to panic.

'Sister, this gun ain't fer fun. It's loaded and I ain't fooling. I've given yer the chance to grab a few things and there ain't no time to lose.'

'Who are you?'

'You'll find out soon enough.'

This strange creature obviously meant what she said. The only thing to do was to obey. Perhaps some of the workmen would be around in a few minutes. She wouldn't hurry — she'd try to gain time. All the same she was scared — horribly scared.

The girl with the gun saw what she was playing for. 'All right. If yer want it that way don't blame me if yer ain't got the things that a dame like you needs when travelling. I got no more time to waste. Sit yer down and write what I tells yer.'

The gun never wavered. This girl did not look mad, but you could not go by looks. Perhaps she'd better humour her. 'Go on — write.'

Elizabeth sat down. ' 'Dear Paw',' the voice went on; ' 'I have been kidnapped. No harm will come to me if Roy McCreedie is released. In other words, it's me for him. If you agree to the exchange, let Glenister McCreedie bring his brother to the foot of the big boulder three miles on the trail east of Twin Forks. If this is not done you will never see me again. If any dirty work is tried, my captors say they will not hesitate to kill me.' Sign yer name,' the husky voice ordered.

'I will do nothing of the kind. My father is a sick man. The shock will injure his health.'

'Very well. Yer've been given yer chance. Leave the note on the table. Come on — pronto. One squeak outa yer and I shan't hesitate to shoot. I'm desperate.'

The girl urged Elizabeth between two

277

freight cars where a rider waited with two spare horses.

'Hyer, Sarah,' he said; 'get a-moving. It ain't healthy.'

The girl pointed to the horses. 'Get up on the sorrel. And remember if we meets anyone, I've still got my gun on yer.'

The path lay through aspen and juniper thickets where mocking-birds sang sweetly from the branches and blue jays screamed at the intrusion. Soon the dark green of the junipers gave way to stunted piñons and the horses' hoofs sank deep into a carpet of last year's nuts and husks. The tinkle of running water rippling through the glades was pleasant to the ear. Chipmunks watched them from overhanging boughs.

The rider who had taken the lead never faltered. Higher and higher they climbed.

The piñons were left behind and now they were riding through tall, dark pines. The air grew colder. The snow-clad peaks of the High Sierras were clearly visible.

Mile after mile they travelled in silence over the wild country. Sundown came and still they kept going. Elizabeth ached in every bone. She was not accustomed to long hours in the saddle. Finally, when she was almost dropping with fatigue, they drew rein at a cabin. She was told to get down.

'If yer give me yer word not to try and escape, I'll not tie yer wrists,' Sarah told her.

Escape! It was the last thought in Elizabeth's mind. She felt as if she could curl up and die. She had never been so tired in the whole of her life.

In no time the man had a fire going. From somewhere at the back of the cabin he produced a battered old coffee-pot and a frying-pan. Soon the smell of cooking filled the room and Elizabeth realized that she was hungry.

It was damp and cold. A couple of rats scurried across the floor and she shrank back in terror. Sarah stood looking down at her with contempt. The firelight made her skin look darker than ever — her eyes showed green and glinting. Her mouth was cruel — a thin straight line, and her vivid lips curled with scorn.

In the whole of her life, Elizabeth thought she had never seen a crueller face.

'I'm darned if I know what any man kin see in a miserable thing like you,' she said. 'You with all yer airs and graces. I reckon I misjudged yer. You ain't got the spine to walk outside that door. You women with yer jewels and yer clothes! Yer mebbe all right in yer fancy boudoirs, but up here an Indian squaw would be a heap more use ter a man.'

She bent over the fire to attend to the cooking. Elizabeth watched her half in fear and half in fascination. She was a strange wild creature. Her slightest movement had the rhythm and grace of a black panther. She used an ordinary hunting knife to turn the meat she was cooking. She produced a tin plate and heaping it generously, she thrust it at Elizabeth.

'Get that down yer. I don't want yer dying on my hands.'

Elizabeth's face must have expressed bewilderment. Sarah gave a jeering laugh.

'What yer waiting for? Some o' those fancy knives and forks folk like yer use? Or mebbe it's a table napkin yer wanting. Use yer fingers, or go hungry.' She went back to the pan and helped the man and then herself.

For a time nothing could be heard in the cabin but the sound of eating. Then Sarah poured out a mug of strong black coffee and pushed it across. It was hot and Elizabeth drank it greedily. It warmed her chilled body and she was grateful for its heat.

When the meal was finished, the man collected the plates and took them outside.

Elizabeth turned to her captor. 'Why do you do this to me? What harm have I ever done you that I should be treated like this?'

Again that jeering laugh.

'Harm! What harm could a helpless critter like you do to me? Don't kid yourself. I'm figgering it's yer carcass they'll value. Yer paw's got influence. If he wants yer back safe and sound he'll bring pressure on the sheriff and Roy McCreedie will be free. If yer paw don't, I'm betting the fella who's loco on yer will.'

Elizabeth Broomfield looked at her in amazement. 'I don't understand you. What man are you talking about?'

'Don't give me that stuff. I ain't denying yer dumb in some things, but yer ain't that dumb. Like everybody else yer knows Glen McCreedie's goofy about yer. Though I gotta admit, now I seed yer fer myself, I can't fer the life of me think why.'

Elizabeth felt the blood rush to her face. She was furiously angry. How dare these people make suggestions which were not true! Not one word of affection had ever passed between her and Glen. She had hated his brutality and his hard outlook on life. Her eyes blazed as she turned on Sarah.

'Whoever told you that story, told you a lot of rubbish. I give you my word that there is nothing between me and the man you mention.'

'Mebbe there ain't. Not on your part. But there is on Glen's. We McCreedies are funny folk and Glen was allus the queerest of the lot.'

'Are you a McCreedie too?'

'Who'd yer think I was? Some wench of a dance-hall gal that Roy'd picked up? Shore I'm a McCreedie — by birth and marriage.'

'You're married to this Roy McCreedie? I'm sorry — extremely sorry.'

'Dang yer ornery hide! You be sorry fer yerself. Yer'll mebbe have need ter be afore I'm through with yer. Roy McCreedie's a man and that's mor'n that sobersides of a brother of his is. And he's my man. We were wed by a preacher mor'n two years ago, in Las Vegas.'

Elizabeth was genuinely sorry for this

wild creature. The prospect of a husband spending years of his life in jail and the possibility that he might be hanged, was a terrible one. Her city-bred mind was appalled by the thought. But the fact that she had expressed sympathy drove Sarah McCreedie into a tempestuous fury.

'Yer sorry fer me!' she screamed. 'That's rich — that is. They'll never send Roy to the Pen. If they do they'll find yer body, sister. I'll see to that if it costs me my life. What will I care? Life up here won't be worth living without him. I made him what he is today, the toughest and most daring owl-hooter of the West. We've lived — lived blame well. Yer ain't no cause ter pity me.' She got up and threw more logs on to the fire.

As the flames blazed up Elizabeth could see the green eyes gleaming like those of a wild animal. Surely this girl was half animal. A shudder ran down her spine. Sarah was talking again.

'We've spent coin like water in

'Frisco, Denver and El Paso. You ain't the only one with fancy clothes. I got my furs and my jewels. And I had a hand in getting 'em. I knows the feel of satin and silk the same as you. But I got mor'n you. I knows the thrill of a race with a sheriff's posse at yer heels. The excitement afore yer sticks up a Bank — the roar of a gun. It's life ter me. I guess I oughta been a man in some ways — not in others. I like ter feel I kin make men do as I tell 'em. It gives me a wonderful feeling o' power.'

She walked to the cabin door and opened it. The moonlight was so bright that the sky still looked blue. The plains stood out straight and black in contrast. Myriads of stars spattered the heavens. One shooting star fell earthwards.

Sarah McCreedie sighed and shrugged her shoulders. 'There was only one man I couldn't mould like clay in my hands and that was Glen McCreedie. His will was allus stronger than mine. I guess that's why I was scared of him. Not the way such as you'd be scared of him

— 'cos Glen would never hurt a woman. I was scared he'd come between me and my ambitions.

'Don't look at me like that!' she snarled. 'I can't help myself. Yes — it was me all right that sent him to the Pen. The day Roy raided the Bank in Ogden, Glen was with me. I meant him to be — 'cos I knew if he'd known our plans he'd have stopped us. He allus was against breaking the law. But we wanted the coin so we could enjoy ourselves. What neither of us figgered on was that Roy would be recognized and that they'd pin it on Glen.'

She laughed again. There was bitterness and a certain sort of triumph in the sound.

'Nary once in the whole trial did Glen open his mouth to give Roy away. All he said was that he was not there.'

Elizabeth stared at her in horror. 'Do you mean to say you allowed an innocent man to be punished for a crime in which he took no part? Why, you could have saved him.' The scorn in her voice seemed to arouse Sarah from her thoughts.

'Shore I did. With him outa the way I figgered Roy'd do as I wanted. Roy wanted me to save him — but I refused.'

Elizabeth could restrain herself no longer. She got up from her chair and faced the half-wild girl.

'You wicked woman!'

Sarah's eyes glared with fury. She struck Elizabeth across the face. 'Shut yer mouth. D'yer think I liked putting him behind bars? But my wants and ambitions came first.' She put her head into her hands — her shoulders shook. 'I can see the way he looked at me when he left the court. I'm guessing he's never seen me since. But I've seen him. He's mild and gentle on top, but he's granite underneath. The Pen could never break his spirit. But Roy's different — it will break him. That's why I'm aiming ter trade yer fer him. The day they put him behind bars he'll have gone from me for ever. I'm taking the biggest gamble of my life.'

Elizabeth had been compelled to listen in silence. Against all her instincts she felt desperately sorry for this untamed creature. Sarah McCreedie was primitive. Primitive in all her emotions — a victim of them. Her protective instinct compelled her to fight for the weaker Roy, and yet allied to that natural affection, she wanted him as a tool for her desires.

'How do you mean,' asked Elizabeth, 'the biggest gamble of your life?'

'I'm gambling on a man I've never understood. If he loves yer as I think he does, he may get Roy outa jail and turn him over ter me. But if he decides ter come hunting fer yer — the world ain't big enough ter hold the pair of us, 'cos he'd trail me to its very end.'

'Why not take me back and see him? I promise to bring all the pressure I can on my father. Perhaps a good attorney could get Roy off with a light sentence.'

'Forget it, sister. I know they'll hang him if I don't spring him outa jail. He was too spry with his gun a while back and a Bank teller died. Besides, I don't trust some o' the gang. When the pressure's put on 'em — they'll talk ter save their necks. And then the law'll be on my trail.'

'Your trail?' Elizabeth exclaimed.

Sarah shrugged. 'I guess so. Yer see, I had a hand in all the jobs we ever pulled.'

'You mean the Bank hold-up and the train robberies?' This was incredible.

'Shore. That was the way I wanted it.' She picked up a blanket and tossed it over.

'Yer'd better turn in. We shall be on the move come sun-up. I oughta make yer do without — I told yer to bring some things with yer.'

'What are you going to do?'

'I guess I'll be all right by the fire. I'm used ter roughing it — you ain't.'

'What about the man?'

'Charlie? He'll be all right. He's on guard with the broncs. He'll sleep when we get to the hide-out.'

For a long time Elizabeth lay on the floor wrapped in her blanket, watching this extraordinary girl who crouched by the fire. She sat close to the dying embers, obviously in deep thought. From time to time she got up and threw more wood on the red glow.

Despite her bodily fatigue, Elizabeth could not sleep. Her mind was whirling like a windmill. Pictures of the events of the last few months chased one another across her mental vision. She had never slept on the ground before in her life — it was cold and hard.

She was worried about her father. Would he understand the note she had been forced to leave? Could he bring any pressure to bear on the sheriff? True, he knew the Governors of the States in which this outlaw Roy had committed his crimes. Would this girl's desperate plan succeed?

She was convinced in her own mind that Sarah was quite capable of carrying out her threats. She would go to any lengths to obtain her husband's release.

Then her mind switched to her own affairs. Was it true that Glen really loved her? He'd never shown it. Yet there was the present of the silver fox furs. Again she wished that she had not returned them.

Would he try to trail her? Perhaps he would not know what had happened. Sometimes he was away for weeks on his search for beef. How wickedly he had been wronged. Her mind went back to the first time she had seen him as he sat with his feet on the rail of the observation platform gazing into the mountains.

She saw him as he dived for the hoofs of that maddened horse, with the Donovan child only a few feet away. The watching crowd had yelled their heads off and the blood was pouring into his mouth from the kick he'd received on his nose. How he had battled with that terrible animal — who could believe that Rocky was the same creature!

She thought of the day when she and

Lyttleton had found him in the hills and given him her father's message. Of how, the next morning, he had pulled up on his beautiful horse outside her father's private car. He must have lavished love and care on Rocky. Yet all this time that terrible injustice must have been rankling in his mind like a black, angry cloud.

She remembered his words: 'The West's all right. It's only when man comes with his lust and greed for wealth, that things go wrong.' Had he ever loved this beautiful wild creature who sat staring into the flames? Had she loved him? Had her greed and ambition killed that love? At last, tired out mentally as well as physically, she fell into an uncomfortable sleep.

The next thing that she knew was that the girl was shaking her. 'Come on. It's time we were moving.'

She scrambled from the hard floor. She could have screamed with the stiffness and soreness of her whole body. Outside the cabin there was a faint suspicion of the coming dawn in the east.

Sarah, hand hooked in belt, watched her as she washed in the stinging cold of a nearby stream. The water refreshed her. Her face tingled. She did her best to get dry on her small handkerchief. When she returned to the cabin a coffee pot was boiling on the fire. After a hasty meal they mounted the broncs and were on their way.

Down canyons and across streams where the water came up to the bellies of their mounts, they made their way. Finally they drew rein.

Sarah took a red bandanna from her neck. 'I reckon from now on we'll blindfold yer,' she said. 'I'm figgering one glade's the same as another ter yer, but I ain't taking no chances.' She tied it around Elizabeth's eyes.

From the gait of her mount Elizabeth knew that they were going down a steep slope. The bronc's hoofs rattled on hard rock, but that was all she could tell.

After some time the bandanna was

removed and she saw that they had stopped in a beautiful valley. It was about two miles long and surrounded by tree-clad slopes and rugged natural ramparts of purple-grey rock.

Here and there brown, white-faced cattle roamed over the valley floor. The luscious green grass with its masses of pink snow flowers, blue and yellow iris, looked for all the world like a patchwork quilt. As they headed for a cluster of cabins in the lee of a high cliff, the toes of their boots brushed against the flowers' heads.

With the exception of two, the cabins appeared to be unoccupied. From these, wisps of smoke wafted gently upwards towards the towering cliffs. Two men appeared.

Elizabeth noticed that the younger was lame and heavily bandaged around his neck.

'Hyer, Sarah!' he shouted. 'So yer pulled it off all right.'

'Shore. It wore as easy as taking candy off a kid.'

The other man, a grizzled old-timer whom she afterwards discovered was the cook, spat in disapproval.

'I'm telling yer I ain't cottoning to this fool notion. Holding up a Bank or robbing a train's one thing. But toting off a young woman like this is plumb crazy.'

Sarah ignored him. 'Get off,' she ordered Elizabeth.

The old man shouted: 'D'yer hear what I said, Sarah?'

The lame man with the bandages answered. 'She'd have to be stone deaf if she didn't.'

The old man planted himself in front of Elizabeth and stared hard at her.

'She's a good looker — mighty purty. But not the sort I'd o' figgered Glen would've gone for.'

'Stop yer yapping and get us some chuck, Unc. We ain't had a square meal since we left.' Sarah turned to Elizabeth and motioned to the larger of the cabins. 'In here, you.'

The inside of the cabin was a

pleasant surprise. It was warm and cosy. A big stove was roaring at one end and the floor was covered with skin rugs. The walls were hung here and there with brightly coloured Navajo blankets. The furniture was home-made, but the rawhide seats of the chairs looked soft and comfortable. The table-top had been scrubbed till it was as white as snow.

Between the blankets on the walls, guns hung in racks. Sarah pointed to them.

'Get them smoke-irons outa here, Boy. I don't trust this dame in spite of her meek and mild ways.'

Elizabeth looked at 'Boy'. She recognized him — it was the young train robber that Glenister had knocked down and disarmed.

The man they had called Unc shuffled in with the food. The three of them sat down to eat. The boy and the old man went and sat by the stove.

The meal was eaten in silence. But Elizabeth could feel the eyes of the two men on her back. She was too famished to mind — never in all her life had she eaten so much.

The old man broke the silence. 'How long yer aiming ter keep her here?' he asked Sarah.

'I've given 'em three days to have Roy by the big rock. And I've told 'em to let Glen bring him,' she answered between mouthfuls of coffee. 'So I figger it's up to them now.'

The old man spat on the stove. 'I reckon the whole notion's plumb loco,' he grumbled; 'I tell yer, Sarah, aught ter do with Glen will put a jinx on us. Three times when he's been around things have gone wrong. First the stick-up on the train, then getting rid o' the cows and now this gold shipment.'

Sarah turned on him like a tiger cat. 'Why can't yer stop bellyaching, yer old varmint?' she snarled. 'If yer'll tell me how we kin get him outa jail when half his gang's with him and the other half dead — well then I'll listen. Right now I'm going ter turn in.' She nodded towards Elizabeth. 'Come on, you. By yer looks yer could do with some shut-eye too. If yer value that purty neck o' yourn, don't get any fool notions about making a break. Yer wouldn't get far in this neck o' the woods. Charlie, yer get inter yer blankets, too.'

'I reckon I'm about ready.' This was the first time Elizabeth had heard him speak. She had been thinking he must be a mute.

Sarah led her into another room equally well furnished. There were skin rugs on the floor, but the bed was only a bunk. It looked soft and comfortable and Elizabeth was glad to throw herself down on it. Within minutes she was fast asleep.

14

Broomfield returned from his survey. For some time he was busy with Grainger in his office. It was near sun-down when he got back to his private car and he was surprised not to find Elizabeth around. Possibly she was a little late getting back from her customary ride.

Suddenly he caught sight of the note on the table. He picked it up and read it. He could not make head or tail of the message — to be addressed as 'Paw' was something to which he was not accustomed. He tossed it back — was it a joke? If so he wasn't amused.

But as it became darker and still Elizabeth had not returned, he began to wonder. That his daughter had really been kidnapped never entered his head. As time passed he began to get worried. He went to find Grainger and Lyttleton.

Enquiries were made — had anyone seen Miss Broomfield? One of the camp cooks had seen her. She was riding with two other folks. Hours passed and still there was no sign of her.

Broomfield sent for Glenister only to be told that he had left camp that morning. His two cowhands had no idea when he would be back.

He must be found. The chief felt that he was the only man upon whom he could rely to handle this affair. Elizabeth was his only child and he idolized her. Since the death of her mother, they had never been parted.

Search parties were sent out, but there was little they could do before sun-up. He ordered steam up in one of the locomotives and returned to Keedie in his private car. He went at once to the sheriff's office, told his story and showed Taylor the note.

The sheriff was sympathetic, but in spite of all Broomfield's arguments, ravings and threats, he remained unmoved. He had no authority to release Roy McCreedie — neither would he do so.

But Theodore Broomfield was not the man to let a mere sheriff stand in his way. Elizabeth meant everything to him. The telegraph wires between three States capitals hummed and the influence and pressure which he brought to bear was successful. Elizabeth Broomfield must be rescued at all costs. The reply was from the Governor of California himself.

The time was getting short — where was Glenister? Broomfield ranted and raved at his non-appearance.

More riders were sent out to look for him. It was like looking for a needle in a haystack. The sheriff would have to take Roy McCreedie to the boulder mentioned in the note.

Preparations were already in hand when the whistle of a freight train coming from the direction of Twin Forks was heard. With a sissing and snorting the train came to a halt on the sidings. Glenister clambered down. The train had brought him and Rocky from fifty miles down the line.

Before he'd had time to unbox the horse he was hustled into Broomfield's presence and Elizabeth's note was thrust at him.

It did not take him long to realize who had thought up the diabolical scheme. It was Sarah's cunning, fertile brain — she was determined to save her husband at all costs.

To think that Elizabeth was in her hands made him shudder. He knew now that he loved this girl. He had done so, he thought, ever since Lyttleton had told him that he owed his job to her.

He looked across the table at the distressed Railroad boss. 'We ain't gotta lot o' time. The person whose hands she's in is no other but my brother's woman. She's been the brains behind every crime they've committed. If he's not released I reckon she'll carry out her threat. If they'll let him go now I'll go after him later myself, in spite of the fact he's my brother. And I'll bring him back to stand his trial.' Glenister's face was grim.

Broomfield looked at him in silence. 'You're a hard man, Glenister.'

'Mebbe I am. But it's the only way I kin see ter get him out of this woman's influence. It's she makes the bullets fer him ter fire. A time in the Pen will either break him or make him. And if I'm any judge, she won't wait fer him.'

'The Governor had agreed to his release,' Broomfield handed over the telegram. 'I'm afraid I've made an enemy of the sheriff, Glenister. But my daughter's safety means more to me than a dozen criminals of your brother's stamp.'

Glen got up from his chair. 'I'll bring her back. I shall need a box car fer the hosses.'

'It will be waiting for you when you want it.'

Glen hurried across to the jail. The sheriff had Roy brought into his office and the brothers met for the first time since Roy's capture. The old conceit and bravado had returned. He jeered as he was brought in handcuffed. 'Didn't I tell yer no jail would ever hold me?'

Taylor was sullen — he did not speak.

Glen looked at Roy with contempt. 'I never expected ter see the day when a McCreedie'd use a woman ter save his neck. I'm wondering what Paw would've said ter yer if he'd been alive.'

'Dang yer, Glen, 'tain't my doings.'

'I know it ain't. It's that female rattler o' yourn. She'll put a noose around yer neck as shore as we're standing here. I'm giving yer fair warning — I've stood all I'm going ter stand from the pair of yer. Brother or no brother, the first sign of trickery and I'll put a slug inter yer. What's more I've given my word I'm bringing yer back ter stand yer trial fer the crimes yer've committed.'

Roy laughed. 'Yer've got yer hands full once I've a gun in my hands.'

'Listen ter me, yer feather-brained fool. I'm giving yer twenty-four hours from the time Sarah hands over the boss's daughter. Then I'm coming after yer. The sheriff here will be with me. As yer brother I'm warning yer fer the last time — get outa the State and don't come back.'

He turned to Taylor. 'Take those cuffs off him, sheriff. And I guess yer'd better come with us to the depot. There's mor'n one fella in this 'ere town that'd like ter put a slug inter him. Where's his hoss?'

'I sent it to the depot.'

Many eyes followed them as they made their way to the waiting train. Broomfield was there to see them off. 'Good luck, Glenister,' he said. 'I'm depending on you.'

It was well past sun-down when Elizabeth woke. She sat bolt upright in the dark. She was terribly afraid. The happenings of the previous day came back to her in a sudden flood of memory. Everything had happened so quickly that it had seemed unreal. But the fact that she was sitting in a bunk in an outlaw's cabin hide-out was real enough.

She lay back and went through all that had happened over again. There was nothing she could do but wait. Somehow she had confidence in Glenister. She could picture him, grim and silent, riding up to the cabins. Her dreams were suddenly interrupted. The door was thrown open. The girl stood there — lighted lamp in hand. 'Chuck's ready. Come and eat.'

This time there were only the two of them and all Elizabeth's efforts to get the girl to talk failed. As soon as they had finished she was hustled back into the bedroom. She heard a heavy bar being dropped into position.

In the morning the old man opened the door and called her out to her breakfast.

'I'm supposed ter shut yer up again,' he told her. 'But I can't figger how yer can do much harm if yer sit out on the bench in the sun.'

She was grateful for the fresh air. From the bench outside the cabin she had a wonderful view of the valley. The new spring green showed up in marked contrast to the darker purple shade of last year's growth. It was a carpet of colour such as only Nature could weave. The snow-clad peaks of the High Sierras lay to her left. From time to time they were blotted out by a heavy white mist. Above there was the bluest of blue skies.

Birds of every variety sang and twittered as they flew among the juniper thickets which made a natural shelter for the cabins. In a nearby corral the horses bucked in sheer joy and raced each other round and round. This was the West that Glenister loved. There was little wonder — she had never seen more beautiful country. It was incredible that such a spot should be the hide-out of desperate men.

She had been so wrapped in her thoughts that she had not realized that the old man was speaking to her. He shuffled his feet a little and she looked up. 'Purty view, ain't it?' he said.

She nodded. 'It's beautiful.'

'Yeah.' He sighed. 'I never gets tired looking at it. But yer should see it in the Fall. There's browns and reds, yellows and greens. Folk talk about the beauty of a rainbow. But ter me it ain't a patch on growing things. Then yer should see it when the snow's on the ground — all white and shiny against the dark green of the laurels and piñons and the black o' the rocks.'

Elizabeth stared at him. What a mixture! An outlaw who had the soul of a poet.

He saw the surprise in her face and he smiled down on her. His face was wrinkled and tanned as dark as any Indian's. His old eyes were still blue — they looked kind.

'Folks think I'm loco,' he went on; 'even Sarah who kids she knows the good things of life. She don't, really. Her with her satins and silks. I once seed a fella with some pictures. He wore a lunger. He shore could put them colours down. I wished I could paint pictures. I reckon them that can bain't ordinary folk. This one weren't. We found him froze ter death in his cabin. He could paint pictures, but he couldn't keep hisself alive.'

Elizabeth could not find anything to say to him. An outlaw who was not only a poet in his ideas, but who also wished he could paint! It was unbelievable.

He was still talking. It was as if he was lonely in some indefinable way and found comfort in expressing his thoughts.

'They tell me, marm, yer knows that other nephew o' mine — Glen?'

'Yes. I know Glenister. So he's your nephew, too?'

'Shore is — and the best of us all. I reckon Glen took after his maw. She had book-learning. Come up here after the war in a wagon train. 'Paches slaughtered nigh on all of 'em. Me and Glen's paw with a bunch o' fellas just come on 'em in time. Us McCreedies allus was wild, but Glen, as I says, took after his maw. He wore quiet and slow, but a hellion when he wore roused. I dun telled Roy and Sarah ter keep outa his way. But they don't listen ter an old 'un like me.'

He sat down with his back against the cabin wall and his long legs stretched straight out in front of him. He pushed his battered old hat on to the back of his head. He was evidently pondering something. Then, as if he'd made up his mind, he turned towards her.

'How'd Glen look these days? I'm figgerin' them three years he wore away he musta gone through hell. And there's no telling what this Sarah will do next. One day Glen's going ter get mad and she'll rue the time she ever did him hurt.

'Will yer tell him from me — but don't let them know — that his uncle Col shore wishes him well. Tell him I'm not so spry as I usta be. The rheumatics got me in the legs and I couldn't hit a barn door with my gun. Me! Colin McCreedie that downed the Seymours!' He stopped. 'I'm sorry, marm,

I reckon I bin letting my tongue run away with me. But it's bin good, talking ter yer.'

He got up from the ground and shaded his eyes with his hand. 'I'm figgering that Sarah and Boy'll be coming back. Yer'd better be going inside — she's a hellion when she starts, blast her ornery soul.

'It's them all right. Look, down there at the end of the valley. Me eyes ain't what they usta be.'

Elizabeth went into the cabin and closed the door behind her. She wondered what her sight would be like when she was his age. The riders had been two or more miles away.

She went into the room with the bunk and sat down on it. The hours dragged by. Sarah came again and called her to eat. After that she was left alone and as the light began to fail she lay down on the bunk — resigned to waiting for another night.

But very soon the door opened again and she was told to get up and prepare

311

for another journey. Outside the cabin the horses were waiting and for hours they rode through the night.

As dawn broke she could see the flat range and away to her right the gleaming railroad tracks, looking like strands of silver on a carpet of green. A few miles away, on the lower ground, a huge boulder stood like a solitary sentinel guarding the trail.

From far away a train whistled. A thin whisp of smoke appeared on the sky-line. Slowly — very slowly to Elizabeth's anxious sight — it came nearer.

She watched the long line of cars coming nearer until with a final puff of steam it came to a halt in a cloud of black smoke. Two figures, minute in the distance, moved away.

From the moment that the train had come to a standstill, Sarah had been peering through a pair of binoculars. She took them from her eyes and spoke to Boy.

'He's there. And there's only Glen with him!'

She had seen two men get down and unbox a couple of horses. 'Go down and meet 'em. If everything's all right wave yer hat twice and we'll follow. Remember, no matter how yer hate him on account of that slog he gave yer in the hold-up, don't try anything crazy. With a fella that kin beat Harper to the draw yer ain't gotta chance.'

Boy swung his bronc around and headed down the mountain. Sarah watched through the glasses. She held them out to Elizabeth. 'Here, yer kin take a look at that heart-throb of yourn. He's still the same as he allus was — cold and aloof. But that's shore a dandy hoss he's riding.'

Elizabeth took the glasses and focused them on the two figures. Even at this distance the two men looked identical. They had drawn rein and were waiting in the shadow of the boulder. She saw Boy approaching.

Sarah held out her hand. 'Here, gimme the glasses.'

The boy had got up to the two men.

He stopped and spoke. Then he waved his hat twice.

'Come on,' said Sarah. 'Don't forget I've still got a gun and I'll use it if things don't go right. Just the same, I gotta hand it ter yer. Fer a gal that wore raised in a city yer got what it takes. I'm figgering this'll be the last time you and me meets. I'll say, though yer been scared ter death, yer never squealed. When yer get back ter the cities mebbe yer'll think of me up here running from the Law. I don't want any of yer sympathy, but you thank the lord yer got what I allus craved for. If yer want yer own life, don't wed Glenister McCreedie. Yer'll never fence him up in a town.'

'Thank you for your advice,' said Elizabeth. 'In return can't I persuade you to give up this way of living? By kidnapping me you may have saved your husband's life this time. But you can't keep running away from the Law all your life.'

Sarah threw back her head and

laughed. 'I guess yer mean well and I'm grateful. But I reckon life's what yer make it. We dun made ours and I can't see me waiting fer no fella fer ten years and that's the least it'll be when they catch up with Roy.'

She kicked her pony into life. 'Come on. They're waiting.'

The two girls rode down the mountain-side in silence.

Elizabeth would never forget the look on Glenister's face as they drew rein within a few feet of one another. His steel-grey eyes looked over her from top to toe and then passed to the girl at her side.

'Hyer, Glen,' Sarah drawled. 'Long time no see. Hyer, Roy.'

But it was to Elizabeth that Glen first spoke. 'Howdy, marm. Are yer all right?'

'Thank you. I am quite well.'

Then he looked at Sarah. 'All right, Sarah, here's yer man. He tells me yer wed. I congratulate yer.'

'Thank yer, Glen. That's shore

mighty kind of yer, seeing how yer hated the sight of us.'

Glen looked her straight in the eyes. 'I'm figgering I have cause ter hate the very name I was born with when the likes of you are around. But I ain't come here to talk about myself. I came to see Miss Broomfield back and ter tell yer that yer had the ace this time. But from now on five aces won't be good enough. I've told Roy yer've got twenty-four hours' start from the time I get back ter Keedie. Then I'm coming after yer and I shan't be alone. So I'm advising yer ter get outa the State.'

Roy McCreedie broke into the conversation. As he spoke Elizabeth noticed how much alike the brothers were. But in Roy's case the firm, strong jaw of the elder was replaced by a weak mouth and chin.

'I told him what ter expect if he gets on our back trail,' he told Sarah. 'But the blame fool says he's given his word.'

Glenister ignored the interruption and addressed his words to Sarah. 'I figger yer the brains behind the outfit. Yer my sister by marriage and I tells yer ter get this galoot outa the State. Head fer Mexico — anywhere so long as yer gets him outa my way. I can't say more. Are you ready, marm?' he asked Elizabeth, and without another word the brothers parted.

When they had covered some distance Elizabeth looked back. Three specks were heading for the mountain trail.

15

The twenty-four hours' grace was up. From the window of Broomfield's private car Elizabeth could see the assembled posse waiting for the train that was to take them as far as Twin Forks where they hoped to pick up Roy's trail.

In reply to their questions she had told both the sheriff and Glenister all that she had seen and remembered of the country over which Sarah had taken her. It was little enough. But she was able to describe in greater detail the valley where the cabins had been built.

To men like Taylor and Glenister who had been born in those parts, the fact that she had been taken through piñons and firs told them that this valley was situated high up in the mountains. Neither piñons nor firs grew below five thousand feet.

She noticed that today Glenister wore two guns. Even she, unaccustomed to the West, knew what that meant. Two-gun men were not common. Those who wore them were usually either desperate men, or men feared by the gun-slicks whose irons were for sale to the highest bidder.

As she stood watching them, her father joined her. 'So Glenister's keeping his word. A hard, but scrupulous man if ever I've met one. It can't be easy for him to go after his own brother. But he gave his word and I guess that's all there is to it for him. I wouldn't like to be in his brother's shoes.'

Elizabeth sighed deeply. Her father looked at her. 'You like him?' he asked gently.

'More than anyone I've ever met.'

Broomfield put an arm round her shoulders. 'You know I'd never stand in your way, my dear, if you told me you loved anyone. But in spite of my admiration for Glenister, I could not honestly say that I should approve of such a match. Men brought up in the rough, as he was, see things from a different point of view. I suppose having to fight for their very existence up here makes them that way.'

'I know. That's what I fear,' she murmured. 'They're so cruel and hard. They never appear to relax for an instant. The fact that they always carry a gun speaks for itself. Look — now he's wearing two. I've heard them say that a two-gun man is either a killer or a bully. I know he's not the latter. About the former, I sometimes wonder.'

Broomfield shook his head. He had his own very definite opinion of Glenister.

'No, he's not a killer. He's a man that I think will go a very long way in this country. He's fearless. He has courage and forcefulness of purpose. The men respect and admire him. Some may fear him. But there's no doubt he can get more out of the workers than any boss I've ever employed. He's saved us thousands of dollars on his beef-buying alone. And what's more the quality's been the best we've had.

'Grainger was telling me that the prospectors over at Rich Bar wanted to give him a valuable claim worth several thousand dollars, but he refused it. Men admire that sort of thing. Undoubtedly he's the most popular man in these parts. He'd go far if he were to take up politics. He'd have the confidence of the people.

'All I hope is that no harm comes to him. Grainger and Lyttleton think very highly of him. In some cases they rely completely on his judgement.'

While they had been talking the horses had been boxed. The posse climbed aboard. The engineer gave the signal and the locomotive pulled out.

'There they go,' said Broomfield. 'I haven't the slightest doubt their mission will fail.'

Somehow Elizabeth found herself hoping that it would. She couldn't explain it for she hated the sight of Roy

McCreedie, and Sarah was nothing but a greedy avaricious woman who would stop at nothing to achieve her ends.

* * *

From Twin Forks the posse headed straight for the big boulder and took up the trail from there. For the first few miles the tracks were plain, but they were lost when the outlaws had obviously ridden down the bed of a shallow river. Water left no tracks and though they spent an entire day examining both banks, not a trace could they find.

They combed the country for three days — the fugitives had gone to ground without leaving a single track. Glenister was puzzled. He was sure that the valley which Elizabeth had described was somewhere around here. And it could not be far off. Sarah and Elizabeth could not have travelled more than twenty miles in one night.

Inwardly he was pleased. He hoped

they'd cleared out of the State — that he wouldn't hear of them again. Personally he was prepared to give up the hunt and several members of the posse shared his feelings.

But Taylor was determined to re-capture Roy McCreedie. His prestige was at stake. His attitude amused Glenister. Night after night men died in brawls and shootings in Keedie and the sheriff seldom worried his head about them. But because Roy had a reputation as one of the toughest owl-hooters, Taylor wanted the kudos of hunting him down.

Close on sun-down on the sixth day of their mission they were in thickly wooded country high up among the piñons. They stopped to make camp for the night.

One of the party had gone off to collect dry wood for the fire. He heard a shot which seemed to come from somewhere directly beneath his feet. He pushed on through the thick scrub. Suddenly the ground dropped away. Below him was a valley — at the far end of it, a cluster of cabins.

He hurried back and reported what he had discovered. Little wonder that they had not been able to locate the place. Scrub and thick undergrowth covered the rim. It was as if the earth's crust had cracked and in that crack had sprung up the lush bunch grass and the sage that Elizabeth had described.

To have located the valley was one thing. But to find the entrance, quite another. It lay three to four hundred feet below them. The cliff sides were almost perpendicular. There was nothing to be done that night except to keep watch. A twinkle of light coming from one of the cabins showed that someone was still around.

At sun-up they combed the rim through mile after mile of dense bush, seeking an entrance and a way down. At last, more by luck than judgement, they found a narrow trail between two large boulders. The rest was easy — they were in the valley. But the open expanse gave them no cover.

The sheriff decided to ride straight for the cabins and take a chance on any possible gunfire. He was no coward. He spurred his bronc into the lead. Glenister rode up alongside him. They must have been all of six hundred yards away from the cabins when a shot rang out — a bullet fell short of them. They had been seen and whoever was there did not intend to give in without a fight.

They drew rein and surveyed the ground. Unless they could make a thicket of junipers which lay to their right, there was not one scrap of cover. The fellow that had built the cabins had seen to that. Another shot fell short. They were out of range.

'What yer make of it, Glen?' Taylor asked.

'We'd better split. Half of us make fer the thicket and the rest fer the corrals yonder. That way we might be able ter wriggle close enough to get a shot at whoever's in there. Otherwise we ain't a chance. They could pick us off like sitting ducks.'

'I aims ter give 'em a hail first.' Taylor cupped his hand to his mouth. 'Hi there, McCreedie. It's no use. Yer had yer chance. Come out with yer hands up. I promise yer'll get fair trial.'

The cabin door opened. Roy stood framed in the space.

'Darn the blame fool,' muttered Glen; 'I give him his chance.'

'Come and get me if yer want me, sheriff,' Roy shouted. 'But I'm warning yer — the first that comes any closer gets a bullet. It ain't us that's worrying none. We got plenty o' grub and shells. So I'm figgering yer wasting yer time. One thing's certain — yer ain't taking me alive. D'yer hear that, Glen?'

'I did,' Glen called back.

'Well, remember, fella, I dun told yer.'

From behind the cabin a figure darted across to the corral. For a moment they were in doubt as to the intention. But not for long. The bars of the corral were dropped and the stock, more than twenty horses, poured out into the valley.

Two of the posse fired and Glen held his breath. Even at that distance he had recognized Sarah. The bullets were a long way short and she made the cabin in safety.

'Now what d'yer reckon they done that fer?' asked the sheriff.

'I figger they got others somewhere around,' Glen answered.

'If yer right, well then, some of us gotta get round 'em. We'll do as yer said. You take half the boys and make fer the thicket and me and the others will take the corral and see if we kin get around ter the back or make that other cabin.'

As soon as they moved a hail of lead came from the cabin. It was clear that Roy was not alone.

'I reckon the best thing we kin do is ter make a bolt fer it,' said Glen. 'Ride like hell when I give the word — NOW!'

He shot Rocky to the front. In no

327

time the gallant grey had covered the intervening distance and they were in the cover which the thick undergrowth afforded.

One of the others had not been so lucky. Another burst of rifle fire had brought the bullets screaming all around. The unfortunate posse man toppled from his mount and lay still.

The thicket gave them excellent cover. But still they were not within good firing range. Some of their bullets reached the cabin windows and they served to give the sheriff and his party cover till they reached the further rails of the corral. From then onwards the fight settled down into a long-range gun duel in which both sides used many shells and did little harm.

'At this rate I reckon we're here for a long spell,' one of Glen's party grumbled.

Another agreed with him. 'I calculate yer right. If those hombres have plenty o' shells, we'll never smoke 'em out.'

Glenister shrugged his shoulders. He

wasn't over keen on the task. There was a woman in there and he hated making war on a female critter. Not that he had any sympathy for Sarah, personally. It was just the principle of the thing.

He saw that the sheriff had got hold of an old buckboard and by knocking some of the corral rails off, he had made it into a kind of shield. Despite the bullets which whistled all around them, they were slowly shoving it along. The bullets could not penetrate the thick corral rails that had been used to reinforce it and it gave them safe cover from which to fire.

This manœuvre gave Glenister's own party a chance to creep forward. They made the best of the opportunity — working their guns till they were hot. But a burst of accurate and deadly shooting from the cabin forced them to retreat, leaving another two men dead.

Glen decided to try to get behind the cabins. At a closer range he would be able to use his gun more effectively. He explained the idea to the rest of the party and crawled to the edge of the undergrowth.

Then, gripping his rifle firmly in one hand, he bent double and raced for the unoccupied cabin. Lead whizzed around him. He felt his hat go. Another bullet singed the shoulder of his coat and a third shot the heel from one of his boots. This last brought him down, but he rolled over and over as he fell and got himself behind the log walls.

He crept cautiously around the back. There was no window or door. No possible means of entrance. The only door faced the occupied cabin from which all the shooting came. He crept to the corner, still keeping under cover, and called out to his brother.

'Give yerself up, yer blame fool, Roy. No matter how many of yer there are, yer can't last fer ever. They'll starve yer, or burn yer out.'

A jeering laugh was the only answer. Roy had barricaded the window with a thick plank table. Every scrap of glass had been shot away.

'Listen, Uncle Col,' Glen heard him calling. 'That's yer favourite nephew telling us ter give ourselves up. Ain't yer proud of him now? A fine McCreedie he's turned out ter be.'

So they'd got poor old Uncle Col with them. Why, he must be nigh on seventy. The last time Glen had seen him the old man was crippled with rheumatism. He'd had nothing to do with the hold-up.

He'd call again. 'Are yer there, Uncle Col?'

'Shore I am. What yer want?'

'Uncle Col, come outa that. Yer've had no hand in these hold-ups. I'll give my word that yer'll be safe enough.'

He tried to attract Taylor's attention. 'Can yer hear what I'm telling them, sheriff? Ain't that right?' But a burst of gunfire coming from the sheriff's party blotted out the reply.

Roy's voice rose above the din. 'There yer are, Uncle Col. That's what his word's worth!'

'I guess I'll stick by my own folks,

Glen,' the old man shouted back.

Glen saw the barrel of a gun come round the edge of the barricading table. He had no idea whose hand held it, but a rifle less was one less weapon for Roy's party and Glen took aim just below the barrel. He fired. There was a yell and an explosion. His bullet must have caught the breech loader.

'You dirty rat,' Roy shouted, and bullets literally rained into the logs above Glen's head.

The light was beginning to fail. Once it was dark the odds would be on the side of the posse — they would be able to move around more freely.

The sheriff's party were blazing away and for the life of him Glen could not understand what they were firing at. Then it dawned on him. They were firing at the stack-pipe of the stove which stuck out above the roof.

He guessed the sheriff's idea. If the stack-pipe were blocked or destroyed the smoke would fill the cabin. The occupants would have to come out or be suffocated. But the notion did not work. The wisp of smoke continued to appear and drift away.

After another sudden burst of fire from Glen's own party there was a squeal of pain. Unmistakably that of a horse. So they had their broncs in the cabin with them!

By this time it was quite dark and Glen wriggled his way back to rejoin the others who had remained under cover in the brush. The sheriff was already with them.

'What yer make of it, Glenister?'

'They got their broncs in with them. I'm figgering they might make a dash fer it.'

'Not they. If they'd aimed ter do that I guess they'd of high-tailed it when they first seed us down the valley. No, I'm aiming ter set fire to that cabin yer wore sheltering behind.'

'If yer do that yer'll be helping them. They'd be able ter see us by the blaze it'd give.'

'Mebbe so. But that cuts both ways

— we'd be able ter see them.'

He detailed two men to make their way over to the cabin and set it alight. The logs were dry — they should have no difficulty.

Glen shrugged. He was not the boss. If it had lain in his hands, he would have taken advantage of the dark to rush them. Blasts of gunfire still poured out from Roy's cabin. He was still on the alert. He showed no sign of relaxing his vigilance.

The two men who had been detailed for the job soon returned. They had found some old blankets, set them on fire and chucked them against the dry wood. Flames were soon coming from the roof. Within half an hour it was a blazing inferno that lit up the whole place.

The sheriff had arranged the posse into two shifts. He had taken the first turn and Glen was due to take the second. Before the second shift was going on duty they were having a spot of chuck.

There was a sudden yell from the sheriff's men as two riders, guns blazing from either hand, came dashing from behind the burning cabin. The sheriff had been caught napping. Before he could realize what was happening the riders had passed him. Rifle fire was still coming from the cabin.

Glenister whipped out his gun. He was on the verge of pressing the trigger when he saw Sarah's wild, beautiful face.

'Hold it,' he yelled to the posse. 'It's a woman.' But he was too late. He saw her clutch desperately at her bronc's mane and then topple forward. The other rider kept on going. He seemed to bear a charmed life. Ducking his head down beside his bronc's neck, he spurred madly on.

To have seen Sarah shot down in this fashion simply knocked the stuffing out of Glenister. Gun still in hand, he rushed over to her. Others followed him. The sheriff shouted frantically for someone to go after the escaping fugitive.

Glen dropped to his knees and looked into the beautiful face. One of the men behind him shouted.

'Holy Smoke! It's a woman.' She had lost her hat in the fall. Her long black hair streamed out on the sage grass. The light from the blazing cabin glinted on it, turning it into strands of shining silk.

The sheriff raced up. He was panting. 'Hell! It's his wife!' he gasped. 'I didn't know she was in there. Come on, get yer broncs, some o'yer. Let's get after him.'

Sarah opened her eyes. She saw Glen. She smiled. And for the first time, the hard, cunning expression that had always been in her eyes had gone.

'He made it?' she asked weakly. 'For the first time in his life he wouldn't listen to me.' She stopped and licked her lips.

'Get some water, one of yer,' said Glen

'It's no use,' she muttered. 'Yer got me twice. I ain't got long. He's away

336

and I made him promise' — again she faltered — 'never ter come back.'

Glen held the water to her lips. He put his hand under her silky hair to lift her head. She coughed. A trickle of blood ran from her mouth. She tried to lift her hand to wipe it away, but she had not the strength. Glen whipped the bandanna from his neck and did it for her.

'Thanks. I guess if I'd let yer do that in the past things wouldn't have worked out as they have. Promise me yer ain't going after him. It was me that was ter blame and I'm paying fer it right now.'

'I promise I won't,' said Glen huskily. 'But the sheriff can't — he's got his job ter do.'

The old fire came back into those green eyes. 'I ain't worried none about him. It wore yer we allus feared.' She gulped as if she were trying to hold back the blood that was again creeping into the corners of her lips: 'Sheriff,' she muttered and her voice was getting fainter, 'Glen, here, never had aught ter do with that hold-up in Ogden. He wore with me. I oughta told the court. So' — there was a long pause — 'long.' She choked and the blood rushed from her mouth.

Glen laid her back gently on to the sage. 'Get a blanket, will yer? She's gone.'

He got to his feet and walked alone into the dark. No one spoke. Their eyes followed him till his figure was lost in the enveloping blackness.

16

Glen never knew how long he had been sitting in the dark of the juniper thicket watching the stars which powdered the night sky.

When he rejoined the others the fighting was all over. The sheriff had gone into the cabin without further opposition.

Boy McCreedie lay dead — his face had been half shot away and Glenister knew that it must have been his hand which had held the exploded rifle.

Uncle Col was wounded, but it was probable that he would recover. The rider, Charlie, had surrendered. The posse had lost three dead, another was wounded.

It was a grim cavalcade that left the valley and headed back to Twin Forks for the train that would take them to Keedie.

The sheriff was the first man to speak to Glenister about his brother. 'I guess yer meant what yer said about not going after him. My Deputy told me what the gal said.'

'Yeah. I reckon the rest's up ter you. Fer three years there worn't a night I didn't go ter my blankets without cursing her name. But I guess her death finished all that. I'd 'a liked ter bury her there. But yer had ter take the body in. I guess I'm through. If our trails tangle again — I mean mine and Roy's — it'll be different. But I'm figgering he's heading fer the border.'

Taylor looked at him in silence for a moment. Glenister looked tired and much older. The lines in his face had deepened. His mouth was set and hard.

'I guess I know how yer feel,' he said; 'and I don't blame yer none. With me it's different. A lawbreaker's a law-breaker and when I took this badge I swore to uphold the Law.'

From Keedie Glenister went to the

camp at railhead. He wanted no further publicity.

For the next three days he busied himself with the routine chores. Something told him it was time to be moving along. He had seen several news-sheets.

Sarah's death and the discovery that a woman had been a member of the dreaded Harper gang, had caused an even greater sensation than the previous disclosure of his relationship to its leader.

Reports from Keedie told of the town being full of newspaper-men. There were also tales of Roy having been seen in half a dozen places in both States.

It was these newspaper reports that Glenister feared. If Roy saw them, he would return. For there was no denying that he had loved Sarah.

The sheriff was already on his trail, but Glen had no doubt in his mind that Roy would give the badge toter the slip. There were thousands of places where he could hide out. He knew the 'badlands' like an open book.

Glen had decided that he would finish the corral and then just fade away. But when he thought of Elizabeth Broomfield he was torn between two emotions. He hated the thought of never seeing her again. But common sense told him that their lives lay poles apart — his fool notions were just pipe dreams.

He had almost finished the corral when the sheriff and a couple of strangers rode up.

'Howdy, Glen.'

'Howdy.'

Taylor appeared to be ill at ease and Glen could not help seeing it.

'What's wrong, sheriff? Have yer picked up Roy?'

'No. It ain't him I come about this time — it's yerself.'

Glen's hand hovered over his gun. 'Now, don't go fer that iron o' yourn. I know yer could out-draw me, but sooner or later yer'd have ter answer fer it. Besides, I don't believe a blame word these fellas have ter say.'

'What have they ter say?'

'Yer Glenister McCreedie?' asked one of the strangers.

'I guess yer knows that without asking. Who might yer be?'

'We're Deputy Sheriffs from Salt Lake City. Some months ago a prison guard was found dead outside Mooney's Saloon. He weren't what yer call a popular figure. There wore nigh on a dozen fellas that had it in fer him. But we couldn't pin the killing on any of 'em. Then Mooney himself comes forward and says he's information that it wore you plugged him. The sheriff checks up and finds it happened the day you comes outa Rocky Point. Then he finds that you and this guard ain't ever been friendly — that yer'd tangled mor'n once. Mooney seems ter know all about yer — tells us yer here. So we comes up ter see yer. Sheriff Taylor tells us how much yer thought on, up here. Else we aimed ter grab yer and take yer back.'

Glen had listened in silence. Here it

was then. Why hadn't he stuck to his feeling that he'd better get moving? However, he wasn't going to take it lying down. They had a long way to go before they grabbed him.

'That yer can't do,' he told them. 'In the first place this is California.'

'Yer wrong there, fella. We gotta extradition order right here.'

'Ain't yer going ter deny it, Glen?' Taylor asked him.

'The killing — yes. But the other's right. I knew Gorman and I hated the bullying rat. I usta share a cage with an old lifer. Gorman took a delight in devilling the poor critter.'

He told them the story of the money and what had subsequently happened. Then it was his turn to ask questions.

'What was the calibre of the bullet that killed him?'

'That's the funny part. It was only twenty-two.'

Glen went on to tell them of Finney and his turning up again in Rich Bar.

The Deputy Sheriffs looked at one

another: 'Somehow,' said the elder, 'I been waiting ter hear Big Shot's name mentioned. There ain't been a killing down town fer years that he ain't been tangled with. But we could never pin it on him. He's shore gotta cast-iron alibi this time, being in the Pen. Well, I'm sorry, fella, but I guess we gotta take yer along ter stand trial. A Penitentiary Guard ain't just an ordinary guy. I figger the jury'll clear yer.'

But they were too late. Glen had his gun out.

'I ain't going back. Don't move, gents. I ain't wanting another killing on my hands.'

'Don't be a fool, Glen,' Taylor pleaded with him.

'I ain't. I'm going ter wring the truth outa Finney if it's the last thing I do.'

Seeing their boss draw his gun, the three cowhands had come at the double.

'Saddle Rocky fer me,' he told them. 'If he's ornery fetch him here and bring me a rifle.'

Taylor could not stand for this with the Salt Lake Deputies there. 'You, there,' he said; 'I order yer not ter resist the Law.'

They just looked at him. 'We ain't taking orders off you, Taylor. Glenister's the boss.'

Glen smiled at the man who had spoken. 'Take their irons, Gus.'

'It'll be a pleasure.'

'I'm sorry about this, Bert,' he said to Taylor, 'but it's the only way I got o' clearing myself.'

'What goes on here?' Broomfield and, of all people, Elizabeth had arrived on the scene. Hastily Taylor explained.

'Put that gun away, Glenister,' Broomfield ordered.

At the same time Glen's man had arrived with Rocky saddled ready for the trail.

'Sorry, boss. But this time I ain't taking orders.'

'Glenister, listen to me. I'll hire the best attorney to defend you if I have to go to New York to do it. If you say you

346

didn't do it — that's good enough for me.'

'Sorry, boss. But I ain't ever going back behind bars and I'm nary giving them the chance ter put me there.'

With gun still in hand he swung himself up on Rocky. 'It's been right good meeting you folks and I enjoyed working fer yer. But I reckon all good things must come to an end some time.'

He turned Rocky. And then Elizabeth acted. She flew to Rocky's side and clasped Glen's boot.

'Please, Glen. For my sake.' The tears were streaming down her cheeks. 'Don't you realize — I love you. If you run away now you'll undo all the good you've done in the past. Please, I beg of you, listen to father. What he said about an attorney is true. If you are innocent of this crime, they can't find you guilty.'

Glenister looked down at her tear-stained face. 'Do yer mean what yer say, marm?'

'You know I do. I think I've loved you from the day you dived at Rocky's feet to save Kathie Donovan.'

He slid his gun into its holster. 'I reckon yer win, fellas. When yer aiming ter start?'

'Thank God you've seen reason, Glenister,' said Broomfield. He turned to Taylor and the two Deputies. 'All right, gentlemen. I'll be responsible for Glenister till you're ready to leave. I'll arrange for a special car to be put at your disposal.'

Glen unbuckled his gunbelt and handed it to Taylor. 'I'm figgering yer'd better take charge of this till I want it again. I'll be ready when you are.'

The next few hours passed far too quickly. Although Glen knew what lay ahead of him, he felt that with Elizabeth's love he could face whatever came.

After a meal in Broomfield's car, during which the chief gave them his blessing, they left for Keedie. From there a passenger train would take him back to Utah. But this latter part of the journey would not be until the next day.

The news that Glenister was in the jailhouse spread like wildfire throughout the town. A crowd began to collect. The numbers grew. The murmur of voices swelled into a roar: 'We want Glenister — we want Glenister.'

17

To make matters worse three work trains pulled in. Bohunks poured from them. Some carried sledge-hammers, others iron bars. 'They ain't having him,' they yelled.

Inside the jailhouse the two Deputies fidgeted with their guns. Taylor walked up and down. Glen lay on his bunk in a cell staring at the ceiling. He was oblivious to all that was going on outside. The fact that Elizabeth had expressed her love for him filled his mind. It was more than he could believe.

Taylor came in through the unlocked door. 'Yer gotta do something, Glen. Else that mob outside's going ter take this jailhouse apart.'

Glen shrugged. 'What yer want me ter do?'

'Show yerself — go out and talk ter them.'

Glen grinned, but he did not stir. 'Shorely yer ain't getting scared none — are yer, Bert? They're only a-showing their feelings. I'd be a blame fool if I tried ter stop 'em.'

'Yer'll be a bigger one if yer don't. Yer says yer innocent. All right then, show it by going out there and giving 'em the low-down.'

Glen swung his spurred heels off the bunk — pushed open the door and walked down the passage to the entrance. He opened the main door of the jailhouse.

As the crowd saw him appear a huge yell went up. He did his best to quieten them. He told them of Broomfield's promise that he should have the services of the best attorney money could procure — that since he was innocent he would stand his trial.

But nothing he could say satisfied them. The only thing they demanded was that he should be allowed to leave the jailhouse. 'We want Glenister — we want Glenister.' The monotonous chant went on.

At last Jim Donovan came to the rescue. He was well on the road to recovery and he pushed his way through the seething crowd. He held up his hand for silence.

'Glen here's my pard. How yer say if he stays with me the night, instead of in the jail?'

A roar of approval came in response. 'So long as he ain't behind bars we don't care,' a spokesman shouted. Jim saw the sheriff. He had no option but to agree.

The following morning an even bigger crowd assembled to see him leave for Utah. Glen stood saying good-bye to Elizabeth. It had been arranged that she should come to Salt Lake City as soon as the date for his trial had been fixed. In the meantime Sheriff Taylor would round up Finney.

Steam was up and Glen had one foot on the step of the car. There was a yell from a work train that had just pulled in. Lyttleton was seen coming quickly towards them. A bunch of folks followed him and in their midst was Railroad Annie. Behind came Cooper and many of the gold claim owners from Rich Bar whom Glen recognized.

'Bring 'em out,' Annie's voice rose above the din. A man whose face was vaguely familiar to Glen was hustled to the front. He was followed by Finney.

'Here, you,' Annie shouted to the Deputies from Salt Lake City. 'Here's yer killer.' She pushed the wretched man towards them.

'But I never intended to,' he shouted. And then Glen recognized him — it was the tinhorn gambler from whom he'd won money in the crap game at Mooney's. But he was still at a loss to understand what Annie was talking about. She turned to Finney.

'Say yer piece, Finney, or there's no trade.'

The engineer of the waiting train blew his whistle, but no one took the slightest notice. Big Shot Finney put on an ingratiating smile.

'Shore now it's all very simple. McCreedie didn't kill Gorman. Mind yer, he had it coming. It was this fella.' He pointed with his thumb over his shoulder to the gambler.

'I'll get yer fer this, Finney,' the man threatened.

'Go on, Finney,' said Annie.

'He didn't mean ter kill Gorman,' Finney continued. 'It was Glen McCreedie he wore after. McCreedie'd won more than a thousand dollars off him and the money worn't rightly his — it belonged to my friend Mooney. Naturally he didn't like losing so much and he fires him and tells him he's no good. The fella wore sore at McCreedie, 'cos he'd knocked him out and taken his gun. Then Glen comes in again that night and he sees him and Gorman go out. So he tails 'em. They wore scrapping with one another and he sees his chance. He takes a shot at McCreedie. He misses and plugs Gorman.'

The sweat was running down the accused man's face. He was trapped like a rat. Lyttleton's crowd were all around him and Annie watched him like a cat watching a mouse.

Finney stood there with a sickly, silly smirk on his face.

'How d'yer know all this?' one of the Deputies asked him.

''Cos I've ways of finding out. When I heard Gorman had got his and the bullet that killed him came from a twenty-two, I knowed it worn't McCreedie. Guys like him don't use toy guns — it's either a forty-four, or a forty-five. I made it my business ter see this guy' — he nodded to the tinhorn — 'and he gives me the low-down.'

'It's a lie,' screamed the gambler. 'He blackmailed me into it.'

Cooper stepped up to the Deputies. He handed a gun to the elder man.

'That's the gun we found on him.' It was a Derringer. Both Deputies examined it. Then they passed it to Taylor. 'A twenty-two all right.'

He handed it back. 'I guess that lets you out, Glenister.'

The crowd cheered, waved their headgear in the air and cheered again. Elizabeth just managed to smile. She was very near to tears from sheer relief. 'Oh, I'm so glad,' she murmured.

The Deputies from Salt Lake City shook hands with Glen. 'No bad feelings, I hope,' said the elder with a wry smile. He turned to the tinhorn gambler: 'Come on, fella. I'm figgering this train's been waiting long enough.' They climbed aboard and the crowd watched them pull out.

Taylor handed Glen his gunbelt. 'Here, fella, I guess yer'll feel more dressed with this.'

Annie pulled a piece of paper from the front of her blouse and gave it to Finney.

'Here's yer blood money, fella. I hope yer satisfied.'

'Thankee, Annie. I am. So long, McCreedie. Mighty glad ter have been of service ter yer.' He disappeared into the town.

Glen looked at Annie. 'And what

might all that have been about?'

She smiled and there was a look of impish glee on her face. 'I give him my Saloon at Rich Bar.'

Glen stared at her. 'Yer mean ter get him ter talk and tell the truth, fer my sake, yer give yer saloon away?'

'That's about it.'

Glen was flabbergasted.

'Annie! How can I ever thank you?'

Elizabeth held out her hand and took Railroad Annie's in a firm grip.

'And me,' she said; 'I can never thank you enough.'

'Shore don't the pair of yer worry none. He's welcome.'

'But that saloon o' yourn was worth a heap o' coin,' said Glen.

'Yeah, it worn't so bad. But' — the impish grin came again — 'Cooper here, just told me they come ter the end of the pay-dirt. I'm figgering Rich Bar'll be a ghost town again before long. I can't rightly figger on who Finney's hoping ter sell his likker to.'

Everyone smiled. The man wasn't

born who'd get the best of Railroad Annie.

'Well, dang my hide,' Taylor chuckled. 'There's no fool like an old fool.'

'Yer've said it,' said Annie. 'And I reckon this calls fer a bang-up celebration and it's on me. So I'm inviting yer, one and all, ter the Line End. And that means you, marm, and yer father.'

Elizabeth looked at Glen. 'I've never been in a Saloon in my life,' she said quietly.

But Annie heard her. 'Well, it's never too late ter start. So come on right now. We're going ter drink the health of the pair of yer.'

18

Spirits were high in the Line End. Broomfield and Lyttleton found themselves being slapped on the back by men who would normally have kept their places when the bosses were around. Elizabeth was radiant, if a little shy in such unaccustomed surroundings.

Glenister felt as if a great burden had been lifted from his shoulders. A few hours previously he had been prepared to head for the 'badlands' and here he was being toasted by all and sundry. He was just about to make his excuses and take Elizabeth home when a sudden hush fell over the entire company.

He heard Annie gasp and Elizabeth cry out. They were looking at the door. Glen turned to see what had startled them. Standing in the doorway was his brother Roy.

His hair was matted — his clothes in shreds. His cheeks were sunken and his eyes bulged. They were not the eyes of a sane man. His hands hung like talons over his two guns. For a second, which seemed like a year to Elizabeth, the only thing to be heard was men's breathing.

Then Roy spoke: 'I've come fer yer, Glen. Yer murdering buzzard.' His eyes glared. It was a terrible scene — brother against brother. 'Yer always hated her,' Roy's voice went on, 'from the very day she showed she preferred me ter you. You! — with yer strait-laced ways!' He laughed and it was the laugh of a madman. He looked round the room.

'Don't any of you others move. I got nothing against yer, but I'll down the first one that does.' He looked again at Glen. 'Yer never did understand her. She took what she wanted and she shore showed me how ter live. And you shot her down. Yer killed the only thing I ever loved. It was you hounded us. Well, I'll give yer what yer didn't give her.' He turned to a man standing next to him. 'Count three. When he gets ter three — go fer that gun, Glen. Yer allus wore a mite faster than me.'

'Roy,' said Glen quietly, 'don't be a fool. Sarah's killing was an accident. You and you only were to blame. I gave yer the chance ter get outa the country. Yer didn't take it. She told me afore she died. It wore her advice ter go.'

'Liar,' Roy spat at him. 'So yer yellow. Yellow in front o' that gal yer aims ter marry. I'm saving her being a widow.'

Elizabeth clutched the bar to save herself from falling. Annie clutched her arm. Roy's voice got shriller. 'Yer'll marry no one. Yer going where yer sent her. Start counting, fella,' he said to the man.

'One — two — three.'

There was a blast. The room smelt of cordite. A thin trickle of white smoke came from the gun in Glenister's hand. He watched his brother's knees make a sort of loop and then buckle. Roy McCreedie slumped to the floor, face downwards. The gun fell from his hand.

Elizabeth saw a faint puff of smoke come from the barrel. Then she fainted.

Glenister lurched and staggered like a drunken man as he walked over and knelt at his brother's side. Eager hands sought to help him as he turned the body over. It was not a pretty sight. Glen's bullet had hit him between the eyes. Those standing near heard him mutter. 'Darn yer. Why did yer make me do it? Yer blame fool. I loved her in the old days as much as you.' Tears came into his steely-grey eyes. It was not pleasant to see a hard, tough-bitten man cry.

Suddenly he lurched and slid to the floor. Then they saw blood on his shirt. Roy had not missed. It was Jim Donovan who ripped the shirt open to reveal a badly shattered shoulder.

'Get a doc — quick, one of yer. Else we're going ter have another dead man on our hands.'

For weeks Glen lay ill in the Donovans' shack. His shoulder was badly shattered — it would never be the same. The doctor had grave doubts if the arm would ever be of any use to him again.

But the main trouble was not his shoulder. It was his soul. For hours he would lie silent and thinking of his brother and of Sarah. Cain killed Abel and lived in purgatory for the rest of his life. Was it to be the same with him?

Elizabeth Broomfield determined to fight for the sanity of the man she loved. Day after day she spent at his bedside till finally a change came over his mental outlook.

He wanted to go to 'Painted Valley' as she had named it. To please him the sheriff had agreed that both Roy and Sarah should be buried there, in the place that they had made their home.

Quietly one morning a preacher called with the Broomfield private car. Glenister and Elizabeth were married. Before the inhabitants of Keedie had become aware of the marriage, they had gone.

The summer passed. Already signs

that the fall was near had begun to show in the woods. Two bronzed riders rode into Keedie — Elizabeth and Glenister McCreedie.

The first to give the news was little Kathleen Donovan. She had recognized Rocky and 'Uncle Glen'.

Both Elizabeth and Glen were radiantly happy. Though the shattered shoulder had left a permanent stiffness, he was otherwise fully recovered. In a week he was back at work.

Another two summers passed. From a peak in the High Sierras he and Elizabeth looked down into Feather River Valley.

The last tie had been laid — the last spike driven in. The gleaming steel rails wound and twisted across glade and canyon. Bridges spanned the roaring rivers. The railroad went its way through the Sacramento Valley into California.

Gone were the construction gangs and the snorting work trains, but the track was completed to remain as a testimony to man's indomitable courage.

The sound of a train's whistle came from afar. Black smoke trailed leisurely across a billowy blue and white sky. Below, a locomotive hurtled on its way, pulling day and night cars to the sunny south and the sea. Another page of railroad history had been written.

They watched it as it disappeared into the Beckwith Pass. Then, happily, they turned their mounts and headed for the wilds of Painted Valley. There in the shade of a gnarled old Cottonwood, Uncle Col tended two graves with loving hands. This was home. A home in the West that Elizabeth had learned to love.

THE END

We do hope that you have enjoyed reading this large print book.

Did you know that all of our titles are available for purchase?

We publish a wide range of high quality large print books including:
Romances, Mysteries, Classics
General Fiction
Non Fiction and Westerns

Special interest titles available in large print are:
The Little Oxford Dictionary
Music Book, Song Book
Hymn Book, Service Book

Also available from us courtesy of Oxford University Press:
Young Readers' Dictionary
(large print edition)
Young Readers' Thesaurus
(large print edition)

For further information or a free brochure, please contact us at:
Ulverscroft Large Print Books Ltd.,
The Green, Bradgate Road, Anstey,
Leicester, LE7 7FU, England.
Tel: (00 44) **0116 236 4325**
Fax: (00 44) **0116 234 0205**

Other titles in the
Linford Western Library:

DAUGHTER OF EVIL

H. H. Cody

When Jake Probyn hauls up outside the Circle F ranch, he's looking for work, not trouble. But he finds trouble in the shape of the boss's daughters and the foreman, Ransome. Things get worse when the old man dies leaving the ranch to his daughters. Then there are back shootings, range fires and one daughter goes missing . . . and while the Drowned Valley on Circle F land has its own eerie story to tell, there's trouble galore waiting for Jake . . .

HIRED GUN

Arthur Lynn

They wait: six riders, rainwater streaming from their hat brims, their Saltillo blankets shielding their ready carbines, the Spur Barb riders are out to kill Dan Bryce, the gun-heavy stranger, hired by the Muleshoe outfit. Bryce will soon be lying dead in the mud, they figure. Bryce's loyalty has been bought, but there's also something there from his past and he has a personal score to settle of his own ... The Spur Barb-Muleshoe war will explode into deadly violence.

THE CAPTIVE

E. C. Tubb

Don Thorpe, a desert-wise Westerner, is asked by General Colman to undertake a mission for the Union forces to find the train laden with Californian gold which would buy arms for the beleaguered South. Don accepts the dangerous mission and on the way to Fort Gorman rescues a beautiful girl and her fiancé from an Indian attack. But then he's captured. How will he escape and betray the South and yet retain the affections of a Southern girl?

RAWHIDE RANSOM

Tyler Hatch

Cole was a good sheriff, maybe a mite too lenient at times, but when the chips were down, the town of Barberry fully appreciated his prowess with guns and fists. But they didn't know there was a tragedy in his past that would affect his actions — until a local boy was kidnapped while Cole was supposed to be guarding him. And the only one who could deliver the ransom was Cole himself.